MW00415629

OPALESCENCE: The Secret of Pripyat

Amaury Dreher

Copyright © 2019 Amaury Dreher

Independently published.

All rights reserved.

ISBN 9781713414117

Translated from the French by Amaury Dreher & Abby Button

To caffeine and wine, my most loyal allies in these nights of writing.

Prologue

25th April 1986

The sun was high in the sky. Calmly, even proudly, it dominated the city.. Cheerful children ran down wide avenues lined with pine trees with flamelike peaks. Their clothes became lighter. A bucolic atmosphere spread, delighting the daily life of the inhabitants. Summer was approaching in Pripyat.

I was 8 years old at the time. Enveloped in childish innocence, I led a peaceful and happy life in this Soviet country, which had seen my birth and childhood.

My father worked at the Chernobyl power plant as a maintenance operator. This nuclear power plant, composed of 4 RBMK reactors with a power of 1000 megawatts was the pride of the USSR. As a symbol of Soviet modernity, it was also the guarantee of Pripyat's prosperity. There, a large number of the inhabitants were bustling to operate the gigantic nuclear complex, while the rest of its population was employed in other strategic sectors such as manufacturing or steelmaking.

The industry was flourishing and the plant was producing the electricity needed for the region. For us, the fission of atoms was crucial. That was our future guarantee. At the time, no one questioned this source of energy, which was so essential to our development. In addition, two new reactors were under construction near the plant, and the huge cooling towers that were elevating into the sky could already be seen.

My father was delighted: the activity was running at full capacity and the promise of a better life was on the horizon. My mother, an industrious and introverted woman, was a secretary at the city hospital. With my little sister on the way, she would soon have a chance to rest. Her name had not yet been decided; my parents couldn't agree, and my father was too occupied to think about it calmly. Every day, he was busy and enthusiastic, happy to go to work. He left the apartment in a meticulous manner, in a well-established routine, his perfectly ironed blue-gray plaid shirt and a few cigarettes in his pockets. A horribly bitter coffee for breakfast was the last stop before his departure. He parked daily in the 400-space car park dedicated to the plant's employees, and went to inspect the gigantic reactor No. 4 to detect and correct anomalies. His role was important, he guaranteed the safety of operations and the proper functioning of equipment. It was one of the components of the vast mechanism that ensured Pripyat's success.

It must be said that life in Pripyat was pleasant. At least by Soviet standards we couldn't complain. Our apartment was cramped, but cosy, and without claiming luxury, we had all the necessary comfort. We would probably have to look for a bigger place to live when my sister was born, but that wouldn't be a problem. My family and I cherished this city.

While Pripyat was originally designed to house the huge workforce that operated the Chernobyl power plant, the city also had a showcase role, as it was supposed to represent the urban modernism of the Soviet Union. Pripyat thus possessed all the contemporary equipment necessary for the well-being of its population: in particular a cultural centre, a cinema and dozens of shops where one could buy all kinds of handicrafts approved by the Party. There was no boredom in Pripyat. Of course, any comparison with a large western city would be absurd. Meat was extremely rare, if not completely absent, the press was not free, and justice was a fantasy. However, progress was beginning. The roar of modernity was not unfamiliar to us.

Education was not to be overlooked: 15 primary schools had been built with a total capacity of 5000 pupils. Along with these, 5 middle schools and a high school completed the system. Maternity, on the other hand, saw the birth of 1000 babies each year; enough to properly supply the population of Pripyat and meet the challenge of demography. Everything had been carefully planned, the high authorities had thought of everything. The city was flourishing and youthful. The average age of its population was estimated at 26 years. A certain dynamism was emerging, suggesting hope for a bright and promising future.

Located 130 kilometres north of Kiev and 17 kilometres from the Belarusian border, the Chernobyl site was chosen for many practical reasons, such as the topology of the area. The nearby river provided cooling for the reactors during their operations and offered the promise of efficient river navigation.

My family arrived in Pripyat exactly seven years ago. I had no memory of my previous existence, of my first trials and errors as a human being. My entire childhood had been spent in this neighbourhood, and shaped by this routine, the contemporary, Soviet way of life that Pripyat was trying to embody. At least that's what we were learning at school. A modern city, for a great country that dominates the world.

Thus Pripyat would be the cradle of a utopia, a beautiful illusion where communism flourished joyfully, without hindrance.

At this time in April 1986, I was looking forward to the imminent opening of the fair. The bumper cars had been installed and proudly displayed in plain view.. There were swings in the parks, ready for use. The famous Ferris wheel had undergone some rotation tests and stood triumphantly in the sky of Pripyat, its small yellow suspended pods attracting the attention of curious onlookers. Everything was ready for the opening in a few days. The kids were ecstatic, , eager to be free.. They dreamed of crowning their childhood with aerial escapades the sky of Pripyat.

26th April 1986

The opening of the fair never took place. Officially, the Pripyat Ferris wheel was never put to use. No children boarded it.

My first memory of the disaster was in a mathematics class. On that ordinary day, I went to school as usual, grumpy and reluctant. The day was clear and cloudless. We were doing a myriad of calculations, each more boring than the next, when someone knocked frantically on the door. I remember perfectly the gravity that shrouded the director's face when he suddenly entered the classroom, interrupting our teacher. Together, they talked at length in the corridor, allowing us a few minutes of improvised mischief and anarchy. Notebooks were flying, ink was spilling, we were madly happy with the lack of authority, a temporary but total freedom.

The teacher finally reappeared at the door, armed with her usual fixed smile. She gave us tablets: *'candies to congratulate us on the work we did during the year'*. The Party was generous, we were happy. These precautions against radioactive iodine were actually intended to prevent the devastating effects of the radiation that was being propagated without everyone's knowledge. The teacher herself was unaware of the seriousness of the situation. She vaguely understood that an accident had occurred and that some remedies should be given out as a precaution. The director had not been generous with details. Panic had to be avoided, security distilled and calm ensured without

11

betraying the secret of the crucial information he held. The Glasnost praised by Gorbachev had found its limits. The rest of the class went smoothly and we were allowed to leave the school.

When I came home from school, I noticed a change of atmosphere in the streets. The morning lull had turned into an almost invisible, but palpable tension. A few adults were acting nervously.. They spoke quickly and loudly, scratching their heads continuously as if they were looking for an answer to an unsolvable problem. The others went about their business without expressing any concern, suggesting that what was going on did not involve them, or was not of any importance to them.

Spurred on by curiosity, I decided to make a detour to the station and approach the edge of the forest where a small gathering had formed. The trees were tall, and blocked my view . I went around the pines and started climbing the hill overlooking Pripyat. In the distance, some kids were clinging to the railing of the bridge that ran over the railway track and was later renamed the Death Bridge. From there, they could see the chaos of the power plant and the gray smoke rising in the sky. The distance may have prevented them from hearing anything, but their eyes remained glued on the relentless cloud of flames and dust. The spectacle , although undoubtedly striking, was also deadly. They were unaware that they were exposing themselves to phenomenal doses of radiation that would not give them a chance. I remained several seconds to observe, trying to find an explanation as if I were one of the adults in charge of the plant. But the smoke made me un-comfortable. Instinctively, I turned around and headed back. I swiftly arrived back at the family apartment.

My mother and I were only alerted of the serious-ness of the accident in the evening after the explosion, al-most fifteen hours later, when my father returned home. He had been woken up in the middle of the night and rushed to the reactor to participate in the operations. Unusually tense, he had rushed to the scene and came back looking exhausted and anxious. He made us swallow new tablets, similar to those in the math class.

'I have to go to the nuclear power plant. I won't be back until tomorrow morning. Avoid going out. And above all, don't open the windows!'

He had spoken these last words in extreme agi-tation. He, who was usually so calm and serene, seemed very worried. It was only later that I understood what had happened.

Shortly after 1:20 a.m., an experiment in the plant had gone wrong. The back-up systems had been deacti-vated and the temperature had risen, causing a chain reac-tion and a phenomenal explosion. Debris from the building was ejected at an altitude of several kilometres. Neverthe-less, the day in Pripyat had gone almost normally, everyone going about their various occupations. The fumes in the sky were objects to fuel conversations, to arouse curiosity at most. Few people were really aware of the seriousness of the events. The kids were joyfully rolling around in the grass as if nothing had happened. In the surrounding countryside, villagers persisted in drawing water and working the land. They had not been warned and were in no way aware of the risks. The object of their labour was now soiled. The land they survived on had become lethal. But no matter what, life went on.

27th April 1986

Around 1:00 p.m. sentence fell. Local radio stations were broadcasting the same message over and over again: *'Warning! Warning! Dear citizens, following an accident at the Chernobyl nuclear power plant, a dangerous level of radioactivity has appeared in the city of Pripyat.'*

The authorities were stingy with information, but they had finally taken matters into their own hands. An exclusion zone was determined. We were forced to flee. The priority was to evacuate Pripyat and the surrounding villages.

During the day, new iodine pills were distributed without further explanation. The authorities had indicated that the inhabitants had to leave and take only the really necessary things; it was only temporary, they would come back in three days and it would simply be an exciting story to tell future generations.

From this point of view at least, the Soviet organisation was exemplary. 1200 buses had been chartered for the operations, lined up 25 kilometres long and ready to take us on board. The logistical feat had worked. It only took 3 hours for the city to be completely evacuated. Fifty thousand people had left their homes without suspecting that they would never return. Would they have fled if they had been aware of the irreversibility of their actions?

Innocent, but not naive, I understood quite quickly that a serious event had occurred. My father was behaving unusually, both nervous and fearful. It didn't seem like him.

My mother sobbed and didn't talk, just packing things, her fingers shaking. I left my toys, books and all my personal belongings. I had to abandon my newly assembled wooden train. The family photo hanging on the living room wall was ripped off, it would come with us. My father stuffed the suitcase with provisions in a hurry. Through his behaviour, I understood that we were fleeing out of necessity and not simply as a precaution.

The other families seemed more serene, almost carefree. They looked like they were taking the evacuation lightly. Some of my friends laughed, the nervous behaviour of the police officers amused them. The panic of the authorities seemed entertaining. I couldn't characterise my emotion. I was observing without understanding. I was interpreting without concluding. My childhood intuition told me I should be very afraid. Despite the general attempts at appeasement, a deep anguish had stirred in me. I looked around180 degrees, slowly scrutinising the stirring of the teeming city. A scent of tension was floating in the air. I was convinced, however, that this was not my last look at these buildings. I would see them again, I was sure of it. In the meantime, we had to flee, rush to safety.

A noise was coming from a building nearby. The trouble was caused by an individual barricaded in his apartment. He stubbornly refused to leave. The neighbours tried to reason with him, but the scoundrel was determined to stay. He was entrenched with a weapon, they said. Some shouted, 'leave him in his madness, he might shoot.' A man more resolute than the others took the lead and broke down the shattered door. He grabbed the rebel, who was petrified with panic, and propelled him outside the apartment to force him into one of the yellow buses. He'd run away like everyone else. The evacuation had to be complete. There were several such anecdotes in the history of this event, but few have been recorded. The moment was unprecedented and uncertain.

Of course, the evacuation order did not only concern Pripyat. The inhabitants of the various villages and hamlets in the surrounding area also had to rely on the exodus. The accident posed a serious risk for miles around, there was no question of compromising local populations. In order to clean up the environment and prevent future contamination, it was also agreed to eliminate animals in the area. Thus, thousands of dogs were brutally slaughtered with the hope that the survivors would not live to spread the radiation. Described a posteriori as genocide by some, this order was nevertheless executed in view of the risks.

Meanwhile, at the power plant, the chaos continued. About 40 helicopters took turns to contain the fierce fire that was constantly breaking out of the reactor core. Given the colossal level of radiation, the pilots had less than ten seconds to position themselves above the target and release their load. Sand, lead and concrete were dropped on the destroyed reactor to counter the flames. The release of radioactive fumes into the atmosphere had to be stopped, but above all a possible devastating nuclear reaction had to be prevented.

However, in defiance of human attempts, cesium 137 was spreading tirelessly.

Radiation is a tough threat: it is invisible, has no taste or smell and emits no noise. It is therefore impossible to locate them without adequate equipment. Our enemy being undetectable, we were totally ignorant of his presence and number. Of course, none of us had a Geiger counter and only the plant staff and some security forces had one. To avoid panic, they did not share any information with us. The secret of the actual state of the disaster was well kept.

The Soviet government waited until Sweden expressed concern on the 28th of April before they officially acknowledged the accident. The Scandinavians had detected abnormally high levels of radioactivity and suspected the USSR. It was finally on the evening of that same day that Moscow announced to the world what had happened. The statement was made through the Russian news agency *Tass*. A simple message was recited by the presenter on television: 'There was an accident at the Chernobyl nuclear power plant that destroyed one of the reactors. Measures have been taken to manage the situation and assistance is being provided to those affected. A commission of inquiry has been established.'

The speech was brief: there was no need to further dramatise an event whose significance no one understood at the time. However, this was not the first disaster related to a nuclear power plant. Previously, incidents had been reported in several countries, including the United States. Nevertheless, the Three-Mile Island accident was not comparable. Chernobyl was making history. The Soviet Union was facing one of the worst crises of its existence and the whole world was watching. The subject was the focus of all European and international news agencies. It hypnotised the ordinary citizens who were suspended in its twists and turns. The Soviet Union was in a delicate situation. It censored information for its own people, but was accountable to the rest of the world.

From the 29th of April, Kiev was off limits to foreign journalists and diplomats. The USSR was trying to avoid the spread of global panic which could be harmful to them. News of overcrowded hospitals and tens of thousands of deaths had reached the ears of several European newsrooms, raising fears and suspicions that would weaken the Eastern Bloc.

Internationally, the reaction was well organised. Many measures were taken, particularly in Poland, the Netherlands and Scandinavia, where it was recommended that children should not be exposed to the outside world, and that they should be administered with certain preventive treatments. In Germany, the panic was obvious and skilfully exploited by some politicians who led thousands of women to seek abortions as a precautionary measure. As for France, the misinformation scandal that shook it is still held today as an example of necessary distrust of the media. While Switzerland was on alert, a French television presenter announced unreservedly that the radioactive cloud had not penetrated the territory and had moved to the German border by some meteorological miracle. Weeks of cacophony followed, and decades of legal proceedings were launched, some of which were only recently concluded.

In the Soviet Union, the fight continued to rage. Although Boris Yeltsin announced the end of the fire on May 5th, 1986, the reactor was not yet out of trouble. The heat inside was still reaching 200 °C, making the containment and assembly of the temporary sarcophagus considerably more complex. In particular, Soviet engineers had been forced to build a huge underground pipeline several hundred metres long to supply nitrogen to be injected for cooling purposes. The challenge was daunting. Men were fighting against a real monster that they themselves had desired, given birth to and feared.

In the years that followed, thousands of workers were sent to the collapsed part of the roof of reactor No. 4 to attempt a major decontamination. The approach was almost desperate, and the means derisory. Each of them had 90 seconds, and no more. The intensity of the radiation was too high, they could die within minutes.

Armed with simple shovels, they had to climb the ladder, do their job while counting in their heads, knowing that a misjudgment would reduce their life expectancy even further. Most of them died in the years following their mission. Others, still alive, had escaped at the cost of disability and incurable illness. Today their struggle has been illustrated by many films and historical documents. A monument has even been erected in recognition of them. Located in the heart of the exclusion zone, it is one of the first stops on the various tourist excursions. Thus the visitor has the opportunity to contemplate a rather confusing gray structure enveloping a replica of the famous evacuation chimney. Liquidators had been carved on the side, armed with shovels, helmets and water hoses. They were anonymous heroes who had been sacrificed at the altar of an apocalyptic emergency.

If there was an unknown episode of this event, it was the trial that followed. In the summer of 1987, plant personnel were forced to appear before a specially constituted court. Foreign journalists were invited to attend the hearings. The process was strictly regulated and their access time was limited. For some, the trial was a farce. Thus, no international observer had the privilege of being present for the entire procedure.

To meet the requirements of the law in force, the trial took place in the exclusion zone, at about fifteen kilometres southeast of the destroyed reactor. The hearings lasted three weeks and left little written evidence. The Board of Inquiry concluded that the staff were negligent and that they had violated the rules and instructions regarding the management of the reactor. Of course, the inhabitants of the Soviet Union were not informed of the progress of the trial. To do so, they had to manage to listen to western radio broadcasts, particularly those of the BBC.

Although the disaster had been investigated, explained and judged, its impact remained unchanged. My family had fled like all the others. The question of returning was never asked.

My father had been on the front line and had been exposed to huge amounts of radiation. He was admitted to a hospital in Moscow where a special unit had been set up to treat the victims of the accident. The facility was over-crowded, the doctors overwhelmed. It was the incurability of patients rather than their number that was the problem. Soviet nurses tried to reassure them with desperate promises and forced smiles. Every day new liquidators were welcomed. They were cared for by their comforting wives. Some cried, others hoped.

My father suspected he was condemned. He had accepted the idea of his own death with almost suicidal ease. Faced with the certainty of the outcome, the doctors allowed him to return to Ukraine. He wanted to see his na-tive land one last time. His fate was sealed, his departure would free up places to receive new wounded. I was con-fused by his courage, but my mother didn't seem sur-prised. She had always known he was like that. Yet she avoided his presence and almost never let him speak of it. Her own condition was deteriorating and she had difficulty with the sight of her dying husband.

In the fall of 1988, he lost the use of his eyes. Medicine had succeeded in prolonging his existence, but his senses were perishing. His cataracts were accompa-nied by rather significant hair loss, bleeding and endless stomach pains. His physical balance was increasingly precarious. He was forced to return to Moscow to that sordid hospital. Doctors gave him three weeks to live. He died two months later.

His death had been anticipated, even expected. He had been one of the first people sent to the site and had been exposed to much higher levels of radiation than the hundreds of thousands of liquidators who later worked on the site. My mother received a medal and decided to bury it in an old chest of drawers. A few years later she married a Viennese architect. For fear of malformation, she had chosen to have an abortion. My sister was never born and I remained an only child, though I longed for a sibling.

For some reason, I gradually lost contact with my mother. Our emotional bond had slowly evaporated. After the age of thirty, our encounters became rarer, more impersonal too, until they became non-existent. Her Austrian husband may have made efforts to accept and educate me, but I had little empathy for him. He was a deceitful being, a manipulator with a voice too confident and teeth too white to be honest. But he was wealthy and enjoyed resplendent social circles, so I had no choice but to consent to his relationship with my mother.

I began my life as an independent adult in self-sufficiency, excluded from any family structure. My step-father had found me a job as a fairly well-paid advertiser. I remembered thanking him with a vigorous but insincere handshake. A few months later, I decided to resign and start a career as a journalist.

I was sent on dull missions, but I was happy with them. That was three or four years ago, I didn't know exactly. Time had passed and had plunged me into a soothing inertia. My life was tiresome, the routine was suffocating me. The boredom of a smooth and dull existence was waiting for me. I would probably end up swallowing Prozac for all my days watching the rain fall through the window. This seemed to be the only possible eventuality.

However, one event managed to turn me away from my daily slump. In 2014, the uprising in Maidan Square revived a sleeping blaze. Like many revolutions, its onset was troubled. Legitimate claims had become violently entangled with dubious motives. Ukraine was in the spotlight of the media, saturating the continuous news channels.

I was following the events with interest. The popular uprising quickly turned into an armed conflict. The belligerents seemed more diverse than they had been at first. Acts of violence were on the increase, as were suspicions of external interference. Bloody images followed one another on a loop. Kiev had caught fire. Condemnation flew in all directions from world bodies and political leaders, along with press releases and attempts at international mediation.

The conflict became too complex for the average viewer, there was no point trying to follow it. In a final programme analysing the events, one of the reporters mentioned the Chernobyl region, where huge works were underway. This allusion captured my heart. In the face of the uproar of the revolution, the other battle in Ukraine had almost been forgotten. The resonance of this name has always had a special meaning to me. The memory of my father, the identity that my mother had tried to deny, the memory that she had hidden from me, all of a sudden seemed to reappear.

My newspaper in Vienna boasted a 'sharp and nonpartisan' editorial line. I suggested to my editor-in-chief the idea of writing a paper on the situation in Ukraine. Faced with the immediate nature of the events and the nature of my origins, he immediately accepted without asking too many questions. I was sent to do a report on this new Ukraine and the so-called split that threatened its population. I had to deal with highly political and sensitive subjects such as the annexation of the Crimea or the war in the Donbass. Ukraine was divided, so was the world. Hard work was on the way.

I was bored with politics. I dared to admit it only too little, but it was only a pretext to going there. Something deeper was driving me to return to Ukraine. An intimate twitch, a kind of imperceptible intuition stretched out my arms. I would go back to childhood lands, abandoned and unknown areas that I wanted to understand. Pripyat had seen me grow up, it was the witness of my young existence. I felt a deep attachment to it. My first memories of being human were rooted there. Not going to Pripyat would be a denial of my identity. I had to go there. Now I wanted to revive that past, lift the veil of my childhood and unlock the secret of my origins. The decision was made. The venom of this crazy idea was spreading too quickly in me.

Damn the Maidan uprising, I would go to the Chernobyl exclusion zone.

FIRST PART

Chapter 1 — Reunions

32 years after the reactor explosion.

A debate was raging in Ukraine over the operation of the plant site. As the Zone was already condemned, should nuclear waste from the rest of Ukraine be stored there? Could Chernobyl become the nuclear wastebasket of the whole of Europe?

Yet brand new photovoltaic panels had been installed 150 metres from the sarcophagus, suggesting a possible healthy conversion. Nevertheless, the lack of sunlight in the region and the low efficiency of the panels left experts sceptical. The project was more symbolic than necessary. The problem of nuclear waste was more urgent. Storage spaces had already been set up before the disaster and their operation continued despite the various maintenance scandals that affected them. The exclusion zone finally seemed to be under control. Radioactivity had fallen and workers from all over the world were present for the work.

The place had taken on a whole new dimension. Once a place to flee, it had now become a curiosity; unhealthy for some, captivating for others. It was said that the Zone was infested with creatures of legend. Double-headed wolves, piglets with deformed eyes and giant ants were supposed to thrive there. The genetics would have gone wild because of the radiation and the natural order would have been disrupted. The Internet was full of paranormal anecdotes and miscellaneous facts about monstrous anomalies that fuelled the imagination of the most naive. Photographs and even pseudo-scientific surveys had been carried out to measure the extent and truthfulness of these myths. For example, a famous American blogger had visited the Zone and published several mysterious photos coupled with dubious stories. One of them was a kind of female ghost wandering around the Pripyat stadium. Obviously, these deceitful actions piqued curiosity, and interest around the Zone grew exponentially. The tourists, more and more numerous, came continuously. They carried the risk of an accident because of their sometimes borderline or even perfectly shameful behaviour.

The Zone had gained the semblance of an amusement park. Visitors, although theoretically supervised, were engaged in activities such as drone races or ascents of the Pripyat Ferris wheel. Some people did not hesitate to handle contaminated objects in order to find the right angle, the proper light to take the perfect picture. A Dutch couple had even promised to marry each other in the small church of St. Elias, a few miles from the power station. In short, things were getting out of hand. Sooner or later, a death would happen. Pripyat's buildings were in danger of collapsing while the stupidity of visitors worsened. Every day the risk increased, raising the spectre of a tragedy. Stalkers' arrests were increasing. There were legions of these lonely prowlers. Some were caught in the act of theft, or burning fires. Drugs and condoms had even been discovered in the crane at the docks. For many, the exclusion zone was nothing more than an escape.

I myself was wondering about this opportunity to go there. Was the picture so bleak? Was it immoral to visit the Zone?

Basically, I knew that my expedition was not really different from those of the Stalkers. I was driven by the same curiosity and found myself indifferent or unconscious in the face of danger. I wanted to see, feel, understand this place that had shaped my childhood and the destiny of the whole of Europe. I wanted to take part in this enigma, to embrace this ode to the vagrancy that attracted so many people.

The exclusion zone was both fascinating and frightening. While the nuclear accident was an undeniable tragedy, it had also had unthinkable positive effects. Radioactivity had defeated human activity, but not wildlife. It was with amazement and satisfaction that the scientists observed an increase in the number of certain so-called endangered species. Lynxes, beavers, wolves and other bears had gradually multiplied in the region. The experts were struggling to understand, to explain the reasons for this prosperity. The inhabitants of the exclusion zone seemed to compromise animal life much more than radioactivity. Cesium 137 was less fearsome than the human species. Iodine-131 was devilishly threatening, but its half-life period was just over 8 days, which made it harmless for the expedition I was planning. According to the scientists, other radioactive elements remained harmful, but I decided to ignore them.

There are several ways to enter the exclusion zone. The first and easiest way is to book a trip with one of the agencies specially approved by the Ukrainian government. Though the proposed excursion is unique in its kind, it remains nevertheless formatted and more or less supervised: the guide who accompanies you has full power over the course of the day. The visitor only follows a pre-established and marked program, much like walking through a large museum with signs announcing the direction to follow. The second option, much more interesting, is the pure and simple intrusion into the Zone in an illegal manner by sneaking through the barbed wire wall and the various breaches it contains. To do this, it was better to have reliable information in order to know the flaws in the gigantic fence. It was also necessary to master the topology of the area and the organisation of military patrols. The operation was risky, which is what made it attractive.

Fortunately, I had a sidekick who would accompany me. I met him at a bar in downtown Kiev. By chance, our conversation had focused on Chernobyl and I told him about my plan to go there.

Oleksandr was a former guide who had decided to quit his job. Vagabonding in the Zone no longer interested him; not that it left him totally indifferent, but he had other plans, other more conventional aspirations notably dictated by his new familial obligations. He had nevertheless agreed to take me and to recompose his role as a guide one last time. Together, we would illegally enter the Zone to cross

Pripyat. I had commissioned him for a brief ride, a few hours at most.

A few days after our meeting he gave me an appointment not far from Maidan Square. I got into his archaic van and headed northwest to reach the exclusion zone. As our project aimed to avoid military checkpoints, we had to drive through numerous fields, taking small routes as old as they were charming.

Oleksandr seemed more and more nervous as we progressed. He knew what was in store for me. The road ended in a modest meadow where we left the vehicle to continue on foot. My companion knew a weak point in the fence, he just had to find it. The breach was delicate, but practicable. As soon as we crossed it, we walked several kilometres. Oleksandr briefed me quickly on the Zone. Various information, figures, anecdotes... He handed me a bright yellow Geiger counter with a fairly modern appearance. 'Keep it with you at all times. Above all, never separate yourself from it. This thing can save your life. Without it you die in the Zone.' I nodded a little fearfully.

We were nearing an abandoned hunter's cabin. Oleksandr indicated to me to stop any further movement. He still had some contacts on this spot. One of his former colleagues appeared behind the wheel of an old battered Jeep. She asked us to get into the back and make us promise to forget about it after dropping us off. We drove for a few minutes, stimulating my impatience even more. While she was driving, I tried to peer through the trees. The light was veiled and made observation laborious. Gigantic spruces followed one another at a dizzying pace. Their spiky trunks intimidated the most reckless of men. They seemed to jealously guard a precious commodity. Already, I felt a niggle of doubt in me. I had to be brave and defy its appeal.

The jeep stopped abruptly. We had succeeded: Pripyat stood in front of us. Majestic and sinister, it challenged our senses. I was looking out, contemplating this vegetative and dilapidated environment. Rust was spreading everywhere. Corrosion progressed like a virus, it extended to all elements of scrap metal and blended gracefully with the moss that also flourished. The ravages of time were omnipresent. Faced with this vision, the heart falters, the mind doubts and reason is tormented. I was looking at a scene that was both ancient and futuristic, optimistic and dystopian. Was it the victory of Nature or the failure of Man?

Oleksandr knew Pripyat very well, he had spent the last twenty years of his life guiding visitors on behalf of one of the best agencies that offered this type of excursion. However, he seemed to feel a certain detachment about the place, contrasting with my amazement, my emotion. For him it was just a huge urban dump, a Soviet ruin synonymous with fresh money where all kinds of young people came in search of thrills.

Oleksandr was born in Kiev, grew up and lived in Poland, and then moved back to Kiev to care for his ageing parents. He had not lived in Pripyat, he could not understand the exaltation that was rising in me as we progressed through the city. He remained indifferent, his arms hanging down, his face indifferent. I even had the impression that he hated Pripyat. Maybe he had traversed it too much. For my part, I had a very special feeling. The place was familiar to me without being identifiable, as if I had been walking through it in dreams for hours, without really ever having seen it. I concentrated on imagining it as my memories allowed. Only flashes came to me, images, scenes of urban life full of activity. I visualised the yellow colour of the buses during the evacuation, the cyclists at the stop, the queues, the then frightened but naive approach of the inhabitants.

Vegetation had proliferated uncontrollably everywhere, blocking space and masking my field-of-view. The calm of the alleys was a decoy. A powerful symphony seemed ready to sound at any moment. It would spring from buildings and trees. Both macabre and triumphant, it would take everything in its path. I fully understood that the post-apocalyptic nature of this environment had been a source of inspiration. The Zone had happily inspired popular culture through many films, series, music and video games, most of which were very well made. The iconic symbols or places of the Zone were taken up and dramatised or even derided.

The evocation of Chernobyl affected every human being. No one remained indifferent. For many, this accident was the ultimate proof of the danger of nuclear power. It was a kind of warning that would have been renewed in 2011 with the Fukushima incident. Chernobyl had become the unstoppable argument of the anti-nuclear activists. It does not matter if nuclear energy had saved millions of lives as a result of its substitution for coal. The radiation graph and associated imaginary had penetrated people's minds and never come out again. Thus, it was easy to fear that all reactors in the world could face a similar fate to that of Chernobyl Reactor No. 4. Hundreds of potentially cataclysmic global threats could occur at any time. We lived in constant fear and had to prevent the perpetual danger of a new accident. And yet, I found myself there, wandering among the remains of this abandoned city.

Silence overwhelmed me with questions, thoughts that swirled around.

Oleksandr wandered casually, hands in his pockets, gum in his mouth. I started a conversation to find out more.

'How many people worked at the plant on that April 26, 1986?'

'I already answered you in the car, officially 600 employees were present on the site on the day of the accident.'

'I guess they all died instantly?'

'Not at all. A handful of them immediately died in the explosion. Just over 100 people were diagnosed with acute radiation syndrome and nearly 30 died in the following months. The others are unharmed. However, many liquidators have developed cataracts while thousands of children have suffered from thyroid disorders. Even today many people are still medically assisted and studied, especially in Belarus.'

'What are we risking by coming here?'

'Nothing at all. Don't worry, not much will happen to you during those few hours here with me. Avoid dangerous places and behaviour. I know the Zone better than anyone. Do you have a place you want to see first?'

'Where is the sports complex?' I asked.

He pointed to a building. Although I had passed it dozens of times, I would never have recognised it. It seemed new to me.

'I'll wait here for you, don't hang around too much, it's very busy around here.'

Unsure of whether his sentence was ironic or not, I headed for the Azure Pool. The famous swimming pool. Now idolised by swimmers all over the world, it was once a commonplace of relaxation, where the youth of Pripyat could enjoy swimming and other aquatic activities. Our parents took us there as often as possible, to relax and let us unwind on weekends. The exercise was important under the Soviet Union, as was the greatness of communist ideology, of which Fizkultura was conceived as a driving force. The bourgeoisie had to be evacuated with fathoms and acrobatic dives. You had to become champions, have a sense of effort and be among the best to represent your country in major international competitions.

I walked through the gym and its basketball court with its dislocated parquet floor. Slightly tense, I cross a doorway to reach the pool. It appeared before me with a shocking suddenness. My stomach began to knot, but I decided to get closer to the edge, remembering my first time there. I had learned to swim in that pool. The smell of chlorine, cold tiles, fog on the windows, the whistle of the lifeguard. These feelings came back to me, possessed me. Moved, I felt the need to touch the small diving board, the only one I had dared to use during my childhood. Stripped of water, the basin seemed larger, deeper, more threatening too. Its walls were decorated with quite ugly graffiti. The vandals had been there too.

Surprisingly, the site did not appear to be any better preserved than the rest of Pripyat's facilities. Indeed, the Azure pool had been abandoned a decade after the disaster; it had benefited from the attendance of workers employed on the damaged reactor and should therefore have been in a much better condition. The workers had been swimming in radioactive water for years. It was only in 1996 that its final evacuation was ordered, as the sanitary conditions were considered too critical. The roof was dilapidated and some parts had already come off. It was only a matter of time before it collapsed. One of the most iconic places in the city would then become a vast pile of rubble and buried memories.

The glass facades obviously no longer existed, yawning gaps had replaced them, revealing an exterior that had previously been invisible due to condensation. Strangely, the clock was almost intact, the hands were present and the red marked dial seemed ready for use. Was it the original? I wasn't sure. Despite an intense effort, I could not remember this detail. My thoughts were interrupted by the vibrations of my phone. It was Oleksandr.

The faithful man was still waiting outside. The message was succinct:

'Come back.'

Disappointed, I reluctantly left the sports complex. I would have liked to linger, remain in this symbolic place and confuse my memories with the present reality. This sudden departure made me want to return.

I arrived outside, my heart a little frustrated, as if I had been torn from a sweet dream at the most critical moment, that of its completion. In the distance already, the evening shadows were disseminating. The trees flickered to the rhythm of the wind and the darkness moved forward.

Oleksandr was waiting for me, slumped against a dying pine stump. He signalled to me that it was time to leave and we walked a few minutes through the forest, following a meagre path around the city. The mysterious Jeep appeared again, this time with another driver and led us to the breach of our arrival. In a hurry and without exchanging a word, we crossed the barbed wire a little like experienced fugitives. It was only once inside Oleksandr's vehicle that he agreed to speak.

'So did you like it? Did you see what you wanted?'

'In part. It was much too short, I wish I had more time. I feel huge potential here.'

'Potential for what?'

'I don't know. To discover, observe, interpret...'

'Are you planning on coming back?' asked Oleksandr, scratching his head, looking thoughtful.

'Maybe. I don't know if that's possible, but I'd like to spend more time there.'

'All right, I could take you there a second time. Maybe we can camp on the site.'

'Oh, really?'

Oleksandr did not answer. He was driving at full speed, spinning his steering wheel much too fast. He wanted to avoid patrols, because we had no authorisation and our expedition was totally illegal. The engine was rumbling and the tyres were squealing. The heating was not working. Outside, the mysterious fog was spreading.

That was the end of my first foray into the Zone. I had only been there for two hours, which felt insufficient and frustrating. I felt like I had sneaked a glimpse of my past, and caressed buried memories. I now wanted to take it and explore these remains. I felt disappointed, I had not entered any building other than the sports centre or visited any neighbourhood. Images were running through my head, building facades, silhouettes of trees. There was so much to see, so much to discover. My brief meeting with Pripyat could not stop there. In Oleksandr's car, I slumped on my seat in an almost religious way, my eyes closed and my hands joined. Absorbed by the silence, I was already planning my return.

Chapter 2 — Touchdown

A few days later. 4:54 p.m., around the Zone.

My GPS was clear, I was less than 300 metres from the breach, the muh sought-after entrance. I had taken care to discreetly note the coordinates in my phone during my first incursion. This time I was going without Oleksandr. I wanted to confront it myself, alone with my memories.

I entered the Zone at night, fed by adrenaline and proudly wearing my infrared glasses. For this little adventure, I had meticulously equipped myself. I had brought a tent, a sleeping bag and various equipment: an HD camcorder and a thermal camera to keep track of my observations, and finally a distress beacon in case I got lost. Provisions too. There was no question of finding a fast food restaurant or picking up contaminated mushrooms. Finally, I had hidden a knife in a secret pocket with the candid hope of not having to use it. No specific itinerary had been planned. I'd improvise.

I walked quickly through the forest, following the semblance of a trail. My steps were not very agile, but determined. They creaked in the snow while my head avoided as best it could the branches that seemed to want to grab me and dissuade me from continuing my journey. I had no fears. The adrenaline and excitement of the broken prohibition ran through my body, diffusing a new and oh so thrilling energy! I didn't know exactly what I was going to do in the area, the important thing was to go there, to see, feel, touch and breathe. So I left without a clear plan. My instincts alone would guide me.

I was thinking of spending two or three nights in the Zone. Probably more. There was obviously no question of sleeping at the Chernobyl Hotel, that hideous building built to accommodate falsely intrepid tourists. I'd go to Pripyat to sleep, like in the good old days.

Contrary to popular belief, the exclusion zone was indeed inhabited, and not only by Babushkas. Administrative staff were responsible for managing the huge territory. There were also technicians whose mission was to watch over the sarcophagus and cleaning operations, but also scientists or simply inhabitants who had chosen to return. As a result, anyone entering the Chernobyl exclusion zone could observe buildings with episodically bright windows where almost normal lives seem to be taking place. According to Oleksandr, the city of Chernobyl even had a bar where a cable TV broadcasted old football matches, all to Maradona's glory. The bart was almost always empty in winter, few workers were present in the Zone at that time.

I walked along the first buildings pretending to look normal despite my outfit. With my strange appearance and equipment, I didn't look like an administrative employee or a forest ranger at all. Anyway, the few souls present didn't pay attention to me. I would blend into the environment as I had imagined. However, things did not go exactly as they had in my previous incursion. Quite quickly, a voice hailed me first in Ukrainian and then in Russian. I had been in the

Zone for less than an hour and a uniformed guard had already spotted me. A threatening tone and harsh words were repeated. I stopped moving and saw an angry man coming to meet me. He was skinny and looked dark. His cheeks were hollowed out while his eyes were surrounded by deep circles. He barked at me as he grabbed his truncheon. I must have frightened him with my black suit and my nervous look. I raised my arms to signify my non-violence. He lowered his weapon and waved at me to approach.

Was it possible to negotiate? Ukraine's extremely difficult economic situation made corruption easy. A few words exchanged and a 50 euro note were more than enough to persuade the soldier who had intercepted me. Despite the smoking ban in the exclusion zone, the guard offered me a cigarette and we left each other good friends. I could go back on the road calmly. The first obstacle was overcome.

I was now warned: I had to be discreet and avoid patrols. The curfew for the Zone was set at 8 p.m. by the authorities. The last groups of tourists had to leave the Zone's perimeter; otherwise the agencies would be subject to heavy fines. My expedition would only be beginning.

Driven by excitement, I trotted through the forest, amazed to be achieving what I had been aspiring to for many years.

With the help of my compass, I tried to head towards what I thought was Pripyat's position. My breath came in gasps, but I didn't feel tired. Here and there, I could see shadows emerging through the mist and snow-storms. Pale, mysterious shapes followed one another, re-inforcing my amazement. Then came the long-awaited contrast. A dark silhouette appeared behind the trees, hint-ing at the proximity of the city. I finally arrived in Pripyat with a racing heart and shortness of breath.

Discovering this place without Oleksandr was much more appealing. A rather prodigious feeling of freedom overwhelmed me. I walked around the city like I was ex-ploring a dream kingdom. The blocks of buildings stood one after the other in true Soviet style. The boulevards of Pripyat were once intimidating. Of course, they did not have the grandeur of those in Paris or Bucharest, but they aerated the city and made traffic flow more smoothly. Thousands of broken windows opened up to my observant gaze. They had sheltered scenes of life, dramas, joys, loves. A little further on, I followed an old bicycle path. Al-most invisible, it was totally devastated by the growth of wild shrubs. No one could have imagined that it had been there, but I was convinced of its past existence. I had cy-cled it many times on my blue tricycle, pedalling at full speed as if to defy gravity and escape boredom.

The night was beginning to fall, the cold was settling quietly, gradually catching me off guard. The fog was back too. I had to find a refuge, a place to sleep. For no specific reason, I chose an imposing building that would serve as a shelter for the night. It seemed high enough to contain many apartments, some of which I hope would be suitable for peaceful sleeping. The elevator was on the ground floor, with its doors wide open, ready to swallow the reckless people who would dare approach it. I preferred to attempt the stairs and started climbing the dusty steps, listening only to the sound of my panting breath. I stopped randomly on the 7th floor of the building, looking for an apartment where I could spend the night in peace. The vast majority of the dwellings were either totally empty or damaged, victims of looting and other prowlers who had degraded the premises over the past thirty years. However, I finally found the Grail: a small hovel with a view of Pripyat and its Ferris Wheel.

The main room was almost bare, but appeared a good place to rest safely. Despite the smells of dust and cement, I almost felt a warm atmosphere, like the one that characterised the return to a home. Children's posters covered the floor. They were illegible and discoloured, but looked authentic. I quietly unfolded my blanket while humming an old Scandinavian tune. I would use my bag as a pillow. I couldn't help but barricade the door in case someone tried to get in while I was sleeping. Reassured, I snuggled up in my sleeping bag, rocked by the regular whispers of the Geiger counter. The night would be chilly, uncomfortable and dangerous. But it didn't matter. I was in Pripyat.

***

In the early morning, I woke up serenely although slightly sore, joyfully attending the early morning show. The sun gradually rose, its rays caressing the surface of the trees. In the distance, the Belarusian peaks could be seen, piercing the few pale orange clouds that accompanied the first rays of daylight. Seduced by this scenery, I almost forgot to restart my Geiger counter.

0.2 microsieverts: the repeated and almost comforting sound signal was back, the day could start.

I promptly repacked and pulled myself out of the room, concerned with leaving no trace of my passage, rushing down the stairs to get back outside.

Pripyat in the early morning was sumptuously calm. Not even the wind could be heard. My senses were not yet fully alert and dreams had not completely deserted my bewildered mind. A certain nonchalance dwelt in me as if I were moving forward on familiar ground.

There was something supernatural about wandering the avenues of Pripyat. This succession of empty buildings, which seemed to be staring at me more than I was at them, created a paranoid feeling in me. The similar appearance of the buildings and the maniacal geometry of the place gave the impression of being in a labyrinth, a post-apocalyptic dream of which I was both the instigator and the witness. The city was not that large, but the growth of trees through the asphalt misled and confused my sense of direction. Winter and its pale shades caused confusion by increasing the contrast in my field of vision. The calm was only upset by the sound of my footsteps in the snow. Light steps, naive steps.

I dreamed of a breakfast while knowing that it was illusory. The berries were contaminated and I wasn't ready to take that risk. I walked my way on an empty stomach, driven by the crazy desire to find the building of my childhood; my first home abandoned more than 30 years ago.

I walked alone through this orphaned maze in search of the cultural centre. The building was easily recognisable, it would be my landmark in this labyrinth. The Ferris wheel that had observed my sleep was no longer distinguishable. I was struck by the atmosphere of the place. Not a single bird was gliding through the sky. There was a striking calm, an almost magical and yet very natural tranquillity. Here, the human senses are disoriented. They who are so used to associating these wide streets lined with buildings with a bustle of activity, with sounds of everyday life, saw themselves here disoriented by strange landmarks, forced to reinterpret the environment around them.

In Pripyat, perceptions are alert, but the mind is relaxed. Silence had found a particular resonance in these snow-covered trees that grew here and there, in defiance of all urban planning considerations, of all human planning. The icy appearance of the surroundings gave the illusion that the city had indeed been preserved despite the passing of time. A telephone booth, Soviet propaganda signs... No doubt about it, time had really broken down in Pripyat. The city had fully preserved its fittings from the 1970s. At least that's what I thought until my eyes distinguished a caricature of Donald Trump painted on an ordinary wall. Thus, Street art had not spared the Zone. Other drawings, quite successful, adorned facades or walls: animals but also radiation graphs. Travellers of all kinds had had a good time decorating the area. The Zone had become their favourite playground.

I couldn't find my apartment. I had been walking around for several hours now without any real purpose. I was hungry and exhausted from the cold. I chose to leave Pripyat and turn back towards the city of Chernobyl, which took me a good hour. I had an inclination to find something to eat. I decided to go to the cafeteria where the workers of the Zone and some tourists ate lunch. Inside, I pretended to be a journalist who had just arrived in search of testimonies for my report. At first, no one really paid attention to me, everyone was focusing on food. This café was basic, but the food was tasty. There was no health risk, because it came from outside the Zone; at least that's what they said. Potatoes, onions, cabbage... No doubt about it, I was in the Slavic country. The workers were happily seated and chatting loudly. All these little people were eating without restraint. Once their bellies were well filled, everyone would return to their various occupations and face the becquerels.

The discussions were lively, there was an atmosphere of open comradeship that stood in contrast to the harshness of the outside world. I was trying to communicate with my neighbours. They were engineers, welders

47

and backhoe loader operators. Their main concern was the containment arch that had been erected only a few years earlier. They described various aspects of their work to me, including the construction of the beast, which had gone on for years. Then it had to be moved over a hundred metres by means of rails specially designed to support such a structure. The challenge had been brilliantly met. The arch was a marvel of engineering and represented the hope of cleaning up the exclusion zone.

The workers worked in rotation. Every fortnight, they left the Zone and enjoyed forced leave. It was essential to limit exposure to radiation and protect the outside world. The project was supported by the highest international bodies. There was no way the liquidators' scandal was going to happen again. Everything had been carefully thought out, planned and executed. Of course, they missed their families. Some had crossed the entire continent to come here. Still others came from Asia or Africa. Overall, they were not afraid and were rather satisfied with their working conditions, which were well above the Ukrainian average. However, as the discussion unfolded, I gained their trust and discordant voices rose. One of them confessed to me halfway that he was not convinced that their safety was fully assured.

'It's a taboo subject here. There are a lot of radioactive leaks. The authorities do not relay them all. Besides, I doubt you've heard of it, but we had a threat of an attack once, from Chechens according to rumours. They wanted to sabotage the arch. We had a massive army deployment for several days to protect us while we were working. The guys were pretty tense. It also seems that Greenpeace is considering actions; whether they'll be symbolic or violent, it depends. Big mouths, those. We've never seen them do anything before. Apparently, they infiltrated some of the units working in the Zone. Confidential photos and descriptions are circulating on the Internet. Reports of radiation leaks, breaches of personal safety, maintenance defects, that sort of thing. The chief was mad as hell. We're very careful now, trying to detect intruders. Our work is too sensitive.'

I nodded, looking innocent. The man took up again:

'At night, things happen that are not clear. There is no doubt that people are venturing into the Zone and doing all kinds of things. Some of them, crazy people, are trying to penetrate the ark.'

'You have no plans to protect the complex?'

'Yes, of course. I can't talk about it too much, but there is a compound, dogs and many other things.'

He stopped suddenly.

'My name won't be mentioned in your article, will it?'

'Don't worry, I'll use a fake one,' I replied with a big smile.

'One last thing: There are places where it is forbidden to walk, and the Red Forest is one of them. The trees are ruined, some pines have been burned by radiation, others have kept an unnatural ruby colour. I suggest you forget it, the forest will get the better of you...'

After these final words, the worker remained silent and turned his attention to the food. I chose to do the same.

Full up, I left the canteen and went outside to continue my exploration. I had approached the most famous of the ghost towns, and I was now intrigued by the villages that surrounded it.

Multitudes of small hamlets were scattered throughout the exclusion zone. Often inhabited by farmers, they had also been abandoned. Thus, like an archaeologist, I spent the day exploring the plains and undergrowth of the Zone, in search of traces of deserted human lives.

In the late afternoon, I arrived in a rather small clearing where unnatural shapes adorned the ground. Pieces of wood, cloth and metal rubble were piled up in a disordered manner, inexorably decomposing . It was probably the remains of a camp of former Stalkers, or even smugglers. The Ukrainian army had probably been reluctant to destroy it, contenting itself with looting what was left of it. Apart from old blankets and empty bottles, there was not much left. No one had come to sleep there for a long time. It was no longer a strategic position, but simply a passage area like any other. However, I managed to find a few old walkie-talkies that were in a half-buried box. I picked one up. It was unlikely that this equipment would have remained in this condition for nearly 30 years. It was an American model, unthinkable in the Soviet Union. The object would have had to have been brought in and left behind many years after the disaster. Some individuals may have slept there recently…

The camp was messy, but intact. It seemed to have been abandoned in a hurry as if its occupants had had to flee. What could the Stalkers have been afraid of? Reclusive in nature, they were not always peaceful when they crossed paths and brawls could break out.

In recent years, the Zone had become a hide and seek ground between the Stalkers and the Ukrainian army. The latter had very few resources, with funds being allocated primarily to the bloody conflict in the east of the country. It was the risk of fire that really worried the authorities, rather than the health of these clandestine explorers. The smoke that would be emitted would release new radioactive particles into the atmosphere which the wind would then disperse throughout Europe. All containment efforts over the past 30 years would be made futile in a single moment. Travelling around the Zone was much riskier in the past than it is today. The harmfulness of radiation was then misunderstood by the local population and the lure of discoveries too high.

In the months following the evacuation of Pripyat and the surrounding villages, thousands of greedy and unscrupulous individuals returned to loot in defiance of morality. Silver, copper, furniture, radios, fabrics… Everything that was transportable became appropriable. All you had to do was help yourself, be the first to get hold of the debris of lives abandoned by tens of thousands of people.

Of course, this windfall aroused jealousy and violence. The looters were often armed and aggressive. Confrontations could break out. Some people took their last breath there, killed by another or eaten away by radiation. At that time, the Zone was a lawless territory where the individuals who were fighting against each other were destined to be forgotten. Certain death was waiting for them. This prospect was obviously only vaguely dissuasive, as there were so many Stalkers entering illegally. However, they were not all solitary. According to reports, some Belarusian and Ukrainian looters were operating in organised groups. They entered the Zone in order to strip everything in their path and sell their findings in the countryside where the populations were the most deprived. They sometimes had a right of way with the army, which closed its eyes. There were many legends about these looters. Simple inhabitants or real organised mafia, it was difficult to characterise them. Some were particularly methodical, meticulously visiting each apartment in selected buildings and taking their belongings. A Russian group was famous in the region. A rumour told of their discovery of an incredible amount of wealth. It was even said that not all of them had managed to extract their trophies from the Zone, but hid them instead so that they could discreetly recover them later and avoid Ukrainian army patrols. A loot was hidden somewhere, buried in the Zone. No one had ever confirmed or denied these legends to me. No one knew the nature of the treasure. Oleksandr seemed so disinterested in the Zone that I hadn't dared to discuss the subject with him.

With my flashlight, I was looking for remains, clues that could inform me about this camp and unlock some of its secrets.

My gestures were measured, almost fearful. I had the impression that I was profaning a sacred place. My eyes were drawn to a black shape near a tree stump. It was a toolbox. I dug it up carefully by clearing the snow and mud from it. The lock was broken, I had no trouble opening it. The objects inside were commonplace for the most part: a few nails, a screwdriver, an English wrench, a rather archaic Geiger counter. The equipment looked American.

I grabbed the counter. Having a back-up device could only reassure me. I powered it with two batteries I had with me. It worked but its accuracy was questionable. Unconvinced, I turned it off and threw it to the ground. The meter provided by Oleksandr would be enough for me.

I slowly walked away from the glade, resting my arms on the snow-covered birches. These first discoveries had whetted my curiosity. I needed more.

I was progressing randomly, improvising my way. I felt that I was getting somewhere, my instincts could not be mistaken. I finally saw a glow through the branches.

It was there, towering and imposing as I had imagined so many times. The sarcophagus glittered in the freezing darkness. It had suddenly appeared in my field of vision like a shooting star, both magnetic and elusive.

Noises of ventilation and busy men were coming out in the distance. The Zone was under video surveillance, but whatever. I approached the gigantic structure stealthily, determined to examine it more closely. This huge dome that contained the famous reactor No. 4 fascinated me.

Once I reached the edge of the forest, I had to walk in the open. I gradually pressed on, glancing furtively around me. Long perimeter walls lined with barbed wire surrounded the complex. I had no intention of entering the sarcophagus anyway. Oleksandr had informed me of the increased risks of such an enterprise. In addition, the place was highly protected, making it really inaccessible.

According to Oleksandr, the installation of the new sarcophagus at the end of 2016 had reduced the intensity of radiation by nearly 90% around the reactor. Indeed, despite the repeated rattling, my Geiger counter displayed 0.20 microsieverts which was a ridiculously low level considering my position so close to the heart of the plant. In order to be perfectly discreet, I decided to disable the device and store it in my pocket. I now proceeded blindly, completely concealing the radioactive danger of my progress.

The sarcophagus enclosure was particularly high-tech, in contrast to the general decay of the Zone. Thus, many motion detectors and infrared cameras were regularly arranged to locate intruders like me. The place was too sensitive, the stakes too high. A further explosion of the reactor and the whole of Europe would be condemned, destroyed by radiation and contamination. Fortunately, the engineers (these modern heroes) had done a brilliant job in designing this huge 11,000-ton steel arch, postponing the problem for later generations.

I tried to get closer, to get around the main entrance. My strides were getting faster and faster, maybe too fast. My feet got caught in a barbed wire knot that the darkness had prevented me from seeing. I fell backwards and shouted a swearword to curb the pain. I was hoping the barbed wire hadn't pierced the flesh, my toe was probably bleeding. Nevertheless, I kept on going, faltering and weakened.

As I progressed, I felt an increasingly sharp pain that spread throughout my entire foot. At last I was forced to stop to take care of myself. The wound had to be bandaged to avoid infection. My bandage was sketchy, but effective. I was ready to go again.

As I got up, I came face to face with a huge, excitable dog. Surprised almost as much as he was, I stumbled and found myself on the ground once again. He started barking and jumping, noisily betraying my position. The intrigued voices men were heard. I had to run. The dog was imposing, but seemed too old to chase me. I hastily fled through the forest, leaving the animal behind me and the silhouette of the sarcophagus evaporating into the night.

Chapter 3 — Apogee

51 ° 18' 19,31" N 30° 03' 57,66" E

Duga was very close, I could feel it. I was heading towards it. I didn't really know how I knew about it anymore. I'd Probably seen it when I was randomly wandering the Internet during one of my periods of insomnia. Its story was surrounded by a rather bewitching mystery. I had to go there and see it.

The Duga site was located about fifteen kilometres south of the city of Chernobyl and was supposed to be a secret and therefore unknown to the general public. Nevertheless, the road was frequently used by military vehicles and maintenance personnel. I had to make my way through the forest in order to remain discreet.

It was a four hour walk, during which I met many deer, lynx and even a wolf. I finally arrived at the site. By that time I felt pretty nervous and impatient.

Soviet propaganda was still visible on the walls of the buildings at the entrance to the complex. There were inscriptions and slogans in the Cyrillic alphabet as well as representations of Soviet officials in advantageous positions inciting admiration and reverence.

Once occupied by hundreds of soldiers and scientists, the complex was now inhabited only by a guard and his dog named Tarzan, a jovial and dedicated German shepherd. Fortunately, the animal was asleep and did not wake up when I passed by. As the area was fenced, the checkpoint of entry was the best way to get there. I crawled on all fours under the window of the small building where the guard was dozing noisily.

Stealthily, I ventured into the complex while holding my breath. There was no question of me waking the sleeping dog. I crossed the compound and entered the forbidden perimeter. I guided my steps serenely towards Duga, whose silhouette rose above the treetops, piercing the pale blue sky with its countless metal rods. I had to progress a few hundred metres on a path along the forest before reaching the thing. The structure was huge. I supposed that in foggy weather it would be impossible to distinguish the summit.

This steel monster, whose existence few people knew about, deserved as much attention as the city of Pripyat. An object of fantasies due to its dimensions and occult character, it produced all kinds of hazy theories combining paranoia, mysticism and secret ambitions. It must be said that the place was intimidating. The radar was up to 150 metres high and nearly 600 metres long. By its size and appearance, it seemed to come straight out of a science fiction movie. Its hidden position in the middle of the forest made it an enigmatic building, a kind of sacred totem. It was the cathedral of Chernobyl, a unique work of which the Soviet Union had perhaps never revealed all the mysteries.

The undeclared objective of such a facility was to detect American-made intercontinental missiles and thus protect the territory from an attack considered imminent by the Soviet staff. The titanic project had disadvantages, the main one being to alter commercial and amateur communications. As a result, European radio broadcasts and air transmissions were affected, causing various disruptions.

From 1976 to 1989, the beast emitted at a frequency of 20 Mhz with a power of 10 Megawatts jamming radio waves all over Europe. Despite the futile protests of private individuals, the radar continued its activity and its defence mission. It was working under great secrecy and with no great impact since no one knew of its existence, and even less of its location. It was only recently that this Soviet military base had become popular in the eyes of the general public. Previously, it was either concealed or falsified by the mention of a youth summer camp on the various maps.

Like the Manhattan Project in the USA, most of the workers on the complex were subjected to a watertight division of labour and were unaware of what was really happening with this machine. Everyone went about their mission without worrying about the more universal plan behind it.

The inhabitants of Pripyat, on the other hand, had lived peacefully a few kilometres away without even having been aware of it. NATO, for its part, was well aware of what was going on there thanks to the many satellite and aerial photos available to its agents. Well, I wanted an aerial view too.

Eager with curiosity, I approached the radar. One of the first ladders of the structure on the North facade had been broken by an intrepid visitor who had wanted to climb far too hastily in order to take a selfie. The unfortunate man had crashed to the ground head first, dragging the metal ladder with him as he fell, as it had not supported his weight and stupidity. Fortunately, there were other ways to get to the top of the radar. I had a plan in my possession that I had retrieved from the Internet. It detailed the different footbridges and ladders that marked the structure. I had briefly studied it before my expedition and had a vague idea of the path I would have to follow.

Some routes were less reliable than others. The Soviet-designed construction had not been maintained for 30 years and had been left abandoned, bound to die slowly from rust and oxidation. It seemed determined to repel that death, however, as the structure seemed stable and solid despite its neglect and the many dilapidations committed by the curious people who had climbed it.

I left my backpack in the snow, also unloading my anorak before starting the ascent. I knew it would be long and painful, but I had prepared for it. I pretended to ignore the rusty colour of the ladder, and tried not to look down.

As I climbed higher, gusts of air made the structure slightly shake, slowing my progress. Battered by the ever-increasing wind, I had to take a break on one of the intermediate platforms that were once used for maintenance and observations. The place was cramped, it wasn't really made for rest. My balance was precarious. Caught by a hasty gesture, I stumbled. Duga's plan fell out of my pocket and flew away in an icy blast, spinning towards the snow-covered forest below. It didn't change my determination, I would persist no matter what. It was time to resume my climbing. My limbs were sore but despite the gusts, I finally reached the upper bridge.

My hands were frozen and bruised. I had no idea how much time had passed, but I didn't care. I had succeeded. This was Duga's summit. From up there, I could see the barracks of the military complex and even some red lights in the distance. It was the sparkle of the power plant and its gigantic sarcophagus.

Sitting on a rusty railing, I watched the sunset unfold across the Zone. My eyes were focused on the horizon, looking at the infinity of the landscape. Thousands of pines surrounded Duga and me, like a huge shield hiding my intrusion from sight. The twilight offered its most elegant finery when the wind had subsided. Very fine snow continued to fall, silently. The first stars began to sparkle. I enjoyed the show for a few minutes. The night was beautiful and cold, I wished it could last forever.

Time passed, and I finally fell asleep. The ascension had exhausted me. I dreamed about a mighty storm. The structure was shaking violently. I felt it collapsing like a house of cards and I stood up unharmed, rising from its deep bowels to face a horde of wretched beings. One of them pulled out a gun and fired at close range. I collapsed among the rubble of Duga, with the black, snowy sky as my last image.

My dreamlike death ended my nightmare. I woke up with a jolt, my forehead sweating despite the cold. The night was now fully settled and temperatures had plummeted. I grabbed my night vision goggles and tried to observe the surroundings. Something was leaping away. It was probably Tarzan, the watchdog. I noticed that he was moving in zigzags, and frequently retraced his steps. Maybe he was hunting a fox? Apart from this confusing movement, it was flat calm.

My watch said 12:40. I was thinking of leaving when headlights suddenly lit up the complex. My pulse accelerated. It seemed to be an SUV that was parking. An individual got out of it. The dog had mysteriously stopped moving.

I hastily tried to put away my night vision goggles. Unfortunately, because of my sudden movement I lost my balance and I was forced to let go of the plane in order to hang on to the railing. The goggles tumbled into the void. I was under no illusions about their fall, they would no longer work. I was now blind. It was impossible to distinguish the silhouette that was moving around down there. I would never know who he was and what he was doing. The vehicle's headlights went out. Perhaps he was also considering climbing the structure? A shiver of anguish gripped me. I didn't know anything about his intentions. I had to run away without further delay.

I decided to start the descent from the back. Secondary routes existed, but according to the Internet they were not recommended because they were unreliable. Nevertheless, I had no choice. I made a quick commitment. My actions were hasty and unconsidered.

I reached the ground in about ten minutes, short of breath and with shaky hands. The calm was astounding. The individual was no longer there. Only the wind turbulence disturbed the tranquillity of the place. Camouflaged by night, I walked to the SUV to try to find a clue. The windows were tinted, it was impossible for me to see inside the vehicle. The license plate was Ukrainian and I couldn't draw any conclusions from it. A frosty wind continued to blow. I had to leave.

As I took a last look at Duga, I saw a shadow climbing up the main ladder. It was the same one I went up when I arrived. His progress was much more assured than mine. The execution of the gestures and their speed were impeccable. Obviously, it wasn't the first time he'd climbed up there. I stood still, spying on the individual's ascension.

He reached the top and settled at the observation post. I realized that he could probably distinguish me too. A chilling breeze prompted me to leave.

I ran away at full speed through the woods. I didn't have the courage to look back. I tried to convince myself that no one was chasing me. I had to stay strong, face this environment, stand up to the Zone.

After a few kilometres, I finally managed to reach a house on the edge of the forest. I was freezing and could hear some hoarse noises. They were male voices intoxicated by alcohol. Slowly, I approached and found myself inside the building. This one was quite spacious and composed of several parts. I was in a kind of living room containing a double bed, a table and some shelves that were quite marked by time. The sounds came to me again, but they were still distant. I was lurking against the wall, watching through the keyhole what was going on. The two individuals were in the other room. They chatted loudly while chewing gum and spoke English with a very heavy, almost growling accent.

'Danny, come over here! It's awesome, there's loads of stuff'

The tall fellow kicked a little wooden horse. His partner was busy rooting around in a cupboard with his fist. He pulled out an old hat covered in dust and put it on his bald head.

'Does it suit me?'

'You look like a bum.'

'Shut the fuck up!'

They giggled and started drinking and chuckling. I studied the smaller lad who was part of the duo. A neo-Nazi tattoo adorned his chubby forearm. He spoke English with a strong Slavic accent. I understood that he was Ukrainian. To make matters worse, he was holding a gun to his hip. Some kind of old rifle he must have inherited from who knows who. His sidekick looked American.

I noticed that their silhouettes were getting bigger. Yes, they were getting closer. I had to get out of here. They were so close that they might see me leave. Instinctively, I chose to slip under the bed. The two skinheads came through the door and threw themselves on the mattress, falling asleep almost immediately. I felt trapped. Their sleep was still light, it would probably only take a sneeze for them to notice me. I made the decision to wait and try to control my breathing to calm down.

It was only when I heard them snoring loudly that I got out from under the bed. I tried to move silently towards the door. The floor creaked, first slightly and then violently. I was being careful to move as gently as possible. But the old parquet floor seemed to moan at my feet. The big Ukrainian fellow opened his eyes and saw me. He got up in a flash and grabbed his rifle. I barely had time to breathe before he shouted incomprehensible words and pointed a gun at me. Confused by the alcohol, he had forgotten that the weapon was not loaded. This reprieve probably saved my life. I ran as fast as I could out of the building and walked away into the forest. In his drunken state he couldn't keep up with me and went back to his sidekick.

Oleksandr had warned me of the presence of these people. Most of them were simply young people who were bored and wanted to spice up their weekends by coming to spend some time in the Zone. Still others belonged to ultra-nationalist movements with well-defined ideas. Russians or Ukrainians, fights often broke out when they met. The conflict between the two countries fuelled their pride. These two, on the other hand, had only brought a shotgun. They had probably only come to have fun in the Pripyat Forest and kill some deer. They were kids, they must have been in their twenties at most. I considered them harmful inconveniences, but I knew they were not my worst threat.

I had no idea that in winter the Zone was so busy. Obviously, these young people were not too worried. They went into the exclusion zone without adequate equipment. They didn't have dosimeters or gloves with them. They dreamed of terror, but they did not have one hundredth of courage of their elders the liquidators, those who sacrificed their lives in the reactor containment operations.

Chapter 4 — Scum

Monday.

I was breaking into a school, the name of which I didn't know. It didn't look like the one I had been at when I was growing up in Pripyat. Would I have recognised it? I wasn't sure.

I moved forward in small steps, almost frightened at the thought of damaging the old parquet floor anymore than it was. Notebooks were strewn all over the classroom floor. Children's drawings were still hanging on the wall. Most of them were torn apart. Some of them were quite successful. All of them were getting mouldy. A German book was open on a page describing animal vocabulary.

Around me, the tables and chairs seemed authentic, ordered as if a lesson had just ended. A yellowish object caught my attention. A brand new little Lego man was sitting on one of the desks with his arms dangling. It must have been brought in and then placed by a photographer in search of inspiration. Unfortunately, this type of travesty was common in the *Zone*. They made the Internet forums happy and many gullible bloggers shared these kinds of clichés. For my part, I was working hard not to change anything. I didn't want to alter this environment that I considered sacred. I snuck between the desks to get close to the closet at the back of the room. It was gutted and revealed a few books, each dustier than the next. Some were covered with inscriptions in the Cyrillic alphabet. These were history textbooks. Dated from 1984, they obviously had not been used much.

With unsatisfied curiosity, I left the classroom and headed for an adjacent room. It seemed to be a teachers' lounge. A crumbling chair was there. It looked much better than the rest of the building, probably because it had been visited less. However, the room was not very interesting, as it was practically empty. The decoration was cold and sketchy, but there were no signs of desecration, which relieved me for a few moments.

I quickly realised that I was not alone. As I was about to leave, I came face to face with a Stalker. He was dressed in a khaki jacket and a gas mask on his shoulder, which startled me. In a fearful reflex, I plunged two fingers into my pocket to grab my knife and brandish it in front of him. The individual raised his arms and told me that he meant no harm. He reached a hand out to me and introduced himself.

Andrei was in his thirties, rather thin, and had bright eyes. His appearance was a little peculiar, half-smiling, half-suspicious. In addition to his blond hair, he had a scar on his left cheekbone, a wound he never mentioned.

We exchanged our experiences, our biographies. He knew the city of Pripyat by heart, but had never entered the Red Forest. He was not very interested in poisonous vegetation. His hobby was urban exploration. The real thing. Not the kind intended to show a Japanese couple around the Pripyat buildings approved by the Ukrainian government.

Andrei visited the Zone frequently, 3 to 4 times a year he explained to me. He felt a real calling to go there, a kind of vital impulse that had to be fulfilled. However, he had no direct connection to the events that had gone on there. Andrei was of Estonian origin and was born in Kiev. Coming from a privileged family, he had not been predestined to wander through radioactive rubble, but rather to study at university and enjoy the capital's trendy bars.

Andrei was atypical. He was trying to escape boredom, to explore buried things. In Pripyat, he had entered the basement of the hospital several times, a place surrounded by stories. 'Not all of them wrong,' he told me, cracking a broad smile. The place was considered by many to be haunted, devoured by paranormal phenomena. We heard all kinds of supernatural stories about it. Despite his encouragement, I stubbornly refused to go there. As well as it being macabre, the levels of radioactivity were much higher in the basements of buildings and I was not yet ready to take that risk. According to him, the Geiger counter had sounded so much down there that he'd had to turn it off so as not to go crazy. To be with oneself only, to falsify the rational in order to tame fear and overcome the anguish of the place: Andrei's stories fascinated me.

We left the building and started walking together while we continued our conversation. He took a small path that wound through the trees. We chatted happily under the icy canopies, almost carefree and unaware of where we were standing.

When he bent down to tie his shoelaces again, I thought I saw the butt of a gun.

'Are you armed?'

'Of course. Not everyone here is benevolent.'

'Have you ever used it before?'

'Only once.'

'What happened? What happened?'

'I was near the Jupiter factory when shots were fired. A bullet suddenly ricocheted a few centimetres from me. I never saw my attacker. As I fled, I tried to retaliate. I could swear I got someone or something. I had to shoot blind, I don't know what I hit. The Zone made me a little paranoid. I don't trust anyone. Don't rely on anyone, not even the military. Believe me, it will probably save your life.'

'What kinds of people have you met in the Zone? Why do they come?'

'As you might expect, most of the visitors here are tourists. They arrive and leave daily in a group with their guide. The rest of the people who are here are working for the Zone. Most are employed by the government and do maintenance. Others are employed by private firms and are assigned to the sarcophagus or to the various nuclear waste treatment centres located throughout the Zone. There are a few soldiers too, although most of them just stay at the checkpoints. Finally, there are the Stalkers. Those prowlers you're now one of. Many of them are attracted to Pripyat's loot. People are poor around here, it's hard to blame them. Some are willing to do anything. Their lives are of little value. I met a young Belarusian man about ten years ago. He was convinced that Pripyat's treasure was hidden in the reactor itself. The loot was bound to be in the most unlikely place. It sounded almost too perfect and too easy. He was so convinced of his reasoning that he devised a plan to enter it. He had asked me to accompany him, but fortunately I declined. I had been able to detect a certain glimmer in his eyes, the kind that inhabits any being possessed by an irrational idea and obsessed with the prospect of its realisation. I knew he would go all the way, no matter what the obstacles.'

'What happened to him?'

'Oh, nothing out of the ordinary. He's dead, nothing more. It's simple, the closer you get to the reactor core, the higher the radiation exposure gets. It's exponential and he knew it. He was aware of the risks, it's all his fault. His body was never returned to his family. It is forbidden to stay in the reactor room for more than a few minutes, the consequences are fatal and irreversible. Who would want to take such a risk? His body was therefore never extracted or formally identified.'

'Did any other people go back there afterwards?'

'Apart from a handful of workers and scientists, I doubt anyone has been there. I heard that a photographer claimed he intended to get in. I don't know what happened to him. People will do anything to make themselves known. With the new sarcophagus, it is even more complicated to enter. The complex is also much better monitored. If you ask me, there's no treasure inside. None at all. It is a Stalker's myth, a fable to make the Zone even more captivating than it already is.'

We walked along the railway, which was heading north. The rail network seemed outdated, but had been renovated in the 1990s. It was now electrified and less abandoned than it seemed. Andrei explained to me that when he spent the night in the Zone he used to sleep on an old abandoned train near Yanov.

'I'll show you, you'll like it.' He pointed it out to me with a big smile on his face.

Together, we followed the steel rails, occasionally crossing different carcasses: skips, tanks and other vehicles. All rusty, all forgotten. Faded signalling equipment still covered parts of the track. However, the railway appeared to be in working order. It had been minimally maintained.

After about twenty minutes, we finally arrived at a small train that seemed more or less preserved. Andrei always had a wide smile on his face.

'This is my hotel!' He exclaimed proudly.

'Do you really sleep here? Isn't it dangerous?'

'It's pretty safe. Animals don't come in and it shelters me from rain.'

The train had been abandoned for about 30 years. The engine looked gray, half-gutted and looked like a pile of decaying scrap metal. The rest of the train was in better condition. Some pantographs were still intact, as were parts of the catenary. Andrei's special carriage was at the back of the train with sky blue walls and red seats. The in-

71

terior was designed like the European trains of the 1950s. The patterns were outdated and the colours dull.

Although Pripyat had become mainstream for explorers, this train was still not very popular. The Stalkers preferred to walk around without spending too much time there. In spite of this, Andrei confided in me that one morning he had woken up without his things. Someone or something had stolen his bag during the night. He hadn't heard anything. With little care, he shrugged his shoulders: 'I'm still alive, that's what matters to me.'

The railway continued and doubled, revealing a second section in much better condition. It crossed the Dneiper River and continued eastward to Slavutych, Pripyat's younger sister, where many people had been displaced after the disaster. The city had been built in a hurry and on a similar model to Pripyat to accommodate refugees. Many workers travelled daily from neighbouring cities to Chernobyl. During the 1990s, the network had been electrified and modernised to provide transport for workers. Rail had played a crucial role in the clean-up operations by transporting men and equipment. In addition, the railway network facilitated the management of nuclear waste buried in the surrounding area. Like visitors to the Zone, workers on the train were subject to daily checks to assess their exposure to radiation.

When we arrived at a switch, we saw a small technical room overhung by a faded sign. It bordered the tracks that separated in several directions, probably towards Belarus. A huge padlock adorned the door, but the glass had been broken. Slowly, I passed my head through the frame. A smell of urine and dust came out, putting me off entering.

Andrei asked me: 'There's nothing in there, I've already checked. Let's get out of here.'

We resumed our walk. As we moved forward, Andrei told me all kinds of anecdotes about the Zone and answered my questions. He explained to me in particular how some Stalkers were planning to organise a concert in the Zone. While small clandestine gatherings had already taken place in the forests around Pripyat, the organisation of an event with a real sound system was not feasible. The authorities would be alerted too quickly by the loud volume. Andrei's dream was therefore to hold a secret gathering in a city building, or even a basement in order to remain discreet. He and his friends wanted to let loose in an exceptional place. They wanted to achieve a transcendence that only the Zone could offer. Andrei had already gathered some contacts of his own. The preparation had to be flawless. For the time being, few details had been formally decided, but the idea was on its way. No alcohol would be distributed. The most difficult thing was to find a suitable place. As almost all the windows were broken, the music would be able to be heard quite easily. Therefore a surveillance system would also have to be set up, people posted on the rooftops of Pripyat would stand guard and take turns. Military personnel would be easily bribed. Only a small number of participants would be invited. I had trouble determining if he was serious or if he was just trying to impress me with his insane plans.

A lightning bolt zapped the sky in a petrifying roar. The atmosphere was becoming gloomy. Torrential rain was falling. Contrary to popular belief, storms also raged in winter and the Zone was not spared.

Andrei took me to a makeshift shelter that was nearby. Consisting only of a cover and a tarpaulin spread out between two trees, our refuge was shabby. But I was confident that it would protect us from the flood. Squatting on the ground, we enjoyed a few cigarettes while watching the ballet of droplets smash here and there.

Smoking in the area is officially prohibited, due to the threat of fire and the dispersion of radioactivity. The Zone was equipped with many sensors and warning systems to prevent such incidents. In winter the risk was low and Andrei told me that most of the detection tools were out of order. With a cheerful smile, he placed a tiny lantern nearby, supposed to give us a little light. Above us, the tarpaulin seemed to struggle not to give in to the pressure of the water. It was strewn with tears and I was not too optimistic about its longevity. The recurring lapping sound and the runoff of drops were soothing anyway.

Using a cup as an ashtray, Andrei began the conversation:

'So you want to go to the Red Forest?'

'Yes, I will probably go there.'

'Are you afraid?' he asked.

'No,' I replied laconically.

74

Andrei winked at me.

'Fine. Don't get lost! No one will pick you up there.'

'Do you ever get scared?'

'Not really. The guys did a good job on the new structure, the Zone is less exposed now. It seems that the old sarcophagus contained more than 150 square metres of cracks. They had to build it in a hurry with robots and helicopters. Can you believe it? It was a total panic. The guys hadn't planned anything like that, it was all improvised. It must have been quite a mess.'

'Yes, I imagine that the population around here has suffered a lot from these issues.'

'Of course. But you know, the Ukrainians are not the most pitiable. The wind dispersed much of the radiation to the North. It is estimated that 20% of Belarusians now live in contaminated areas. Almost a quarter of the territory is infected indefinitely. I mean, it doesn't interest the western media.'

'I have read that some reports question the impact of the accident on health?'

He shrugged his shoulders.

'Yes, it's hard to know, there are not many studies available. We are only beginning to have the necessary perspective. The World Health Organisation and the United Nations concluded that the consequences of the accident were overestimated.'

'Haven't cases of thyroid cancer exploded?'

'They have increased, that's true. But that is also due to the fact that the medical follow-up of the population has been much more thorough than before, so more illnesses have been recorded. You know, radiation has a cataclysmic connotation. The truth is that in some parts of the world, such as China, the United Kingdom and Iran, some people are exposed to much higher levels of radioactivity in natural contexts. The biggest victims of the disaster were the liquidators, those who were sent in from the very first moment.'

'What about the inhabitants of the exclusion zone? I heard that some of them are still living here.'

'Yes, many of them have returned, including the Babushkas. These grandmothers are the real Chernobyl rebels. But they are not at much risk today. People like us even less so.'

'I am very intrigued by the Babushkas... Have you already met some?' I asked.

'Of course, there are not many more and they are quite scattered, but you can find them quite easily. Although, almost all of them are close to the end. They've been here a long time, you know.'

'When this century is over, what will happen to the Zone? Do you think it'll lose its aura? Is the Zone immortal?'

'I've been thinking a lot about the posterity of this place. Of course, the sarcophagus is planned for a period of 100 years, but what should we do next? Should a third enclosure be built? Will science have made enough progress? Some are already imagining the construction of a giant dome that would cover a large part of the exclusion zone. The future holds the promise of better materials, and new technologies to solve the problem. Scientific progress is our lifeline. We cling to it as a comforting and unverifiable hope. Neither you nor I will be there to admire the result. I believe that the Zone will be eternal, but subject to permanent control. The danger will always be present, but controlled and contained.'

'Are the Stalkers doomed to disappear?'

He shrugged again, pulling on his cigarette.

'They will be forced to renounce. I guess they'll just have to observe the Zone from the outside. Maybe they'll develop ploys to get in. Some will probably have the crazy idea of digging tunnels. They will emerge on the other side of the ramparts thanks to their radioactive underground routes and any effort to keep them out would be in vain. Employees working for the Zone will continue to be corruptible. What's the point of sacrificing so much energy to lock down this space? It will never be inviolable. It never was.'

Andrei did not say any more words. He was confined to looking into the void and remaining silent until I called him out:

'Tell me, what do you do when you're not in the Zone?'

'Oh, nothing interesting. I am content to live,' He soberly asserted.

Cigarettes were running out and the cold was gradually settling in. Under-dressed as usual, I was soon shivering. Andrei had noticed my discomfort. He plunged his head into his bag and almost miraculously took out two vials of Nemiroff. Eager to lose our cares, we worked hard to exhaust them. Though my companion seemed unaffected by the sweet nectar, I for my part swigged on with increasing enthusiasm; a sign that my judgement was deteriorating. The tarpaulin would hold up. So would my liver. I grabbed the small bottle of Nemiroff and downed it. The feeling of fullness was amazing. I was now ready to spend the night outside, to sleep without fear.

The lantern was dimming, the darkness would soon envelop us. Feeling my eyelids getting heavy, I took one last look at Andrei. He had fallen asleep silently, his arms wrapped around his bag in a somewhat tragic posture. I closed my eyes.

We were woken up by the first light of day. My sleep had been short, but deep. Slavic spirits had played their part magnificently in my dreams, one epic following another. I had dreamed of being a warrior at the head of a Viking army, ready to strangle anyone who stood in my way and prevented me from protecting my own. My dream was disconnected from the Zone, as if my subconscious mind refused to acknowledge it. My alcohol-infused imagination had numbed my limbs and fogged my mind. I struggled to get up.

Andrei was already standing up, laying out an apple that he had carefully cut up. He winked at me and added: 'I picked it up outside the Zone, it's safe to eat.'

Once we'd eaten our breakfast, we tried to carefully pack our belongings and gather our rubbish, removing all traces of our passage. We were getting back on the road.

Andrei was jovial, he whistled as he walked. 'I will show you something. It's one of my favourite places in the Zone.'

It wasn't far: a huge warehouse full of irradiated vehicles. The employees of the exclusion zone had placed the various devices there, which had been mobilised in the first moments of the disaster. As soon as their mission was completed, they had to be shut away because of their radioactivity, which was considered too high. They were no longer usable and had no other purpose than to be stored until they were forgotten.

The gate was blocked by inscriptions and dissuasive signs. A heavy lock had been installed to keep out intruders. However, there was a ladder on the north face, so it was easy to climb up and reach the roof. From there, it was possible to get in through an air duct and then sneak into the various garages.

Andrei handed me a mask. It was essential to limit our inhalation of dust and gas emissions, the nature of which I generally preferred to ignore. The passage also had a foul smell which we had to get accustomed to.

We crawled to a kind of desk with multiple empty shelves. The light in the room obviously didn't work anymore, so I turned on my headlamp. There were some mouldy filing cabinets and piles of rubbish which released an abhorrent smell. We decided to go out and down the stairs to reach the basement. All kinds of vehicles were there. They were perfectly aligned, as if their owners had wanted to display them in an excessively immaculate manner. The garage was much larger than it seemed from the outside. It had several floors, including an underground part housing larger models. Buggies were stationed at the upper levels. One of them seemed to be in excellent condition.

'This thing still works, doesn't it?'

Andrei replied to me in a blink of an eye.

'Officially no one has used it for 30 years!'

I approached a small van with a Soviet logo on it. I tried to peer through the glass, but a thick layer of dust blocked my view. Andrei asked me: 'Above all, don't touch anything. This dirt could be very harmful.'

Beer cans were perishing in a corner. The darkness was sometimes contrasted by meagre rays of light. Rebellious, they would sneak between the gaps in the wooden planks that were supposed to block the windows.

Andrei moved carefully, with a meticulous and observant eye. He was looking for something. He explained to me that he had installed a motion detector on his previous visit. 'I've always been curious about the number of people who come in here. This place is much less well known than Pripyat. Access is considerably more difficult. But that has not prevented 16 people from entering since last year.'

He finally located the small box, hidden next to a toolbox. He inserted a new battery into his device and carefully replaced it. The detector was calibrated to detect only human presence, animals weren't registered.

'Why don't you film it?'

'The darkness makes it impossible to install a traditional camera.'

I offered him my thermal model. We discreetly covered it with tyres and various equipment that was lying around. My camera could last for several weeks and was connected by satellite, so we would be able to view it remotely and know who was prowling around here.

Satisfied, we tried to get out of the building and into the delicate passage through the ventilation duct. I was relieved to be in the fresh, pure air again. The toxic particles I had probably been breathing could have polluted my lungs and reduced my life expectancy by several months.

Andrei seemed indifferent. He was used to adapting to these kinds of challenges and had had to overcome much worse. I observed the way he moved, the way he looked. He seemed to know every corner of the Zone and always seemed able to find familiar landmarks.

As I spent more time with Andrei, I began to grasp his personality. He was neither a looter nor a daredevil in search of thrills. He defined himself as an authentic protector of the Zone. He wanted to observe it, to understand it, to defend it. He was a kind of forest ranger who looked after the exclusion zone as if he had a mandate to do so. It was his garden after all, his escape.

Andrei questioned me: 'So, what's your opinion on nuclear power?'

'I'm not the greatest expert on the subject. It seems that power plants keep causing serious problems around the world.'

'Yes, recently in Japan... But technology is not to blame. These engineers did not correctly anticipate the effects of a tsunami on the reactor. Now the ocean is partially contaminated and hundreds of thousands of people have been displaced. According to the experts, evacuations were superfluous, but people would not have accepted a contrary decision. You know, specialists no longer have the confidence of the general public. Though it's unfortunate, I understand them. This technology is beyond them. They don't realise how much it has brought them. Obviously, nuclear fission is not the perfect process, it is only a transitional step towards even greater progress, replication of the sun using nuclear fusion!'

'Isn't it moving too quickly? More and more powerful, more and more complex... I imagine the risks are also increasing?'

'Not at all, but here again, we just have to trust the experts.'

'So Chernobyl will never happen again?'

'Chernobyl is an unprecedented ecological and human disaster, but we could face much worse. Much worse...'

Andrei was scratching his chin, looking both thoughtful and terrified.

'What are you thinking about?'

'Oh, you see, there is a...'

At that moment an alarm sounded. A powerful spotlight came on, flooding us with blinding light. Our cigarettes must have activated some sensors and the Zone's warning systems had activated. Our indolence was quelled. Andrei pulled me by the arm. 'Kneel down and come this way.'

He led me to a small ditch below. Both of us flattened ourselves and tried to avoid any movement. Above us, the sounds of breathless men were heard. They were looking for us. The guards were rushing to where we had been a few minutes before. One of them shouted to give us up. Andrei laughed.

'They're really not very talented.'

'Why do you keep smoking in the Zone if you know the risks?'

'I do what I want here, I am at home,' he replied dryly. 'The Zone is mine.'

His eyes were bright when he spoke these last words. This demonic glow that emanated from his gaze made me uncomfortable.

'Let's leave,' he ordered.

'I'm following you.'

Behind us, the men were shouting and seemed angry. Obviously, this was not the first time this kind of situation had occurred. As we fled through the woods, I understood one thing: Andrei was looking for this type of confrontation. He liked to torment authority, defy rules in dangerous conditions and emerge victorious with a final twist only beknown to him. He was above all a player, he loved to test human characteristics and expose weaknesses. I thought that one day he might repeat this behaviour towards me. I had to be on my guard, not to trust him more than he deserved. Already, I felt a certain paranoia inside me, precisely the one he had warned me about.

The night was clear and cool, unclouded. The stars were perfectly visible. I couldn't read them, but apparently Andrei was able to decipher them because he was adapting our route accordingly.

'We've left the sensitive perimeter, they won't look for us here, no matter what we do.'

I nodded as a sign of approval.

'So you've never been caught?'

'Never,' he replied, not without some pride.

'I was intercepted by a soldier from day one.'

'If they're alone, you can bribe them. A lot of Stalkers have been through this.'

'That's exactly what I did.'

'Be careful, however, many of them have integrity. I don't want to have to pick you up from a Ukrainian jail.'

'Do you know any people who fell into trouble?'

'Of course. That being said, it was a long time ago.'

'What happened?'

'Stalkers died,' he replied laconically. 'A big fight broke out a few years ago, most of them were drunk. Finally, the army intervened and took the wounded stragglers on the spot. They hanged themselves in their cells. Families sued, implying ill-treatment, but the investigation showed that this was not the case. I think they were out of their minds.'

'I have the impression that many people come out of here with their minds a little disturbed.'

Andrei had a diabolical little smile.

'There's still time for you to go.'

At these words, I remained quiet for a few minutes. I finally broke the silence:

'Are we going to spend the night here?'

'Oh, no, come with me. I know a camp nearby.'

'What? A camp?'

'Yes. At this time of year, it is almost deserted. But it's not so bad, we'll be more discreet.'

He chose the opposite direction to the one I would have taken.

We made our way through tall grass. It tickled our faces as we progressed. The ground was muddy and the snow seemed dirty. I wondered who would have had the idea to settle in such a place. I was not disappointed when we arrived. A small wasteland extended with a single tent within it. It was lying down miserably against a tin shack. The smell was pungent.

'It's there!' Andrei exclaimed with a smile.

He started to scatter his things and set up our shelter while I was inspecting the area.

'What does it look like in terms of radiation?'

'Don't worry about it! If you worry about that constantly, you won't sleep at night.'

The sound of footsteps was heard. The owner of the already assembled tent was arriving. He had a slow gait and wore a huge coat that covered him heavily. All he needed was a sceptre and he would have looked like a druid.

'Here's a new one,' he muttered.

He had spoken these words with a hoarse and muffled voice, suggesting heavy consumption of alcohol and cigarettes.

Andrei introduced us.

'How long have you been living here?'

'It has been about fifteen years now,' replied the individual.

He spat on the ground.

'And I am not about to leave,' he continued.

Andrei intervened:

'Egor is a prowler. He's a vagrant, he goes, he comes. He knows everything hereabouts...'

'It's okay, I think he understands who he's dealing with,' Egor said. 'What are you doing around here?'

'We triggered the alert systems because of our cigarettes,' Andrei replied. 'The smoke betrayed us, but they didn't get us.'

The tone of his voice showed a certain pride that seemed to annoy Egor.

'I see.'

He turned to me.

'What the hell are you doing here?'

'I'm a journalist, I'm doing a report on the Zone and those who explore it.'

Egor frowned and groaned. He did not appreciate my answer and seemed suspicious. Andrei noticed it and tried to calm the situation.

'Don't worry, he won't stay very long and I'll always be with him. We can trust him. Isn't that right?'

He winked at me.

Egor coughed loudly, sputtering phlegm everywhere. He muttered a swearword and began to clean his jacket with his hands. Andrei gave me a sneaky, somewhat embarrassed look. Egor finally managed to calm his cough and spoke again.

'Tell me Andrei, are you still hanging out with Oleksandr? That crooked dog!'

'Do you know Oleksandr?' I asked, turning to Andrei.

'Everyone knows him here,' Egor replied. 'If I see him, I'll break his jaw.'

He shifted himself while spitting on the ground.

'They had a little disagreement,' Andrei breathed to me. 'Oleksandr is very discreet right now. I don't think he is interested in the Zone anymore, and prefers to spend his time in Kiev with his family.'

Egor growled like a bear, before ruffling his shaggy beard, scattering the ice crystals that had lodged in it. He then coughed violently, creating a kind of respiratory eruption, expelling gunk everywhere.

'He's better off staying there,' he replied, wiping the muck off his chin. 'Oleksandr is a jerk, I'd kill him if he ever decided to come here.'

Andrei was looking to lighten the mood:

'Tell us Egor, how many years have you been walking the Zone?'

'Alas, too many, but it's my fault. I've grown too fond of it to give it up. It is true that time erodes what little remains of it, but I will never be tired of it.'

I noticed that Egor was holding a flask of alcohol in his large, hairy hands. It was a cheap vodka, with no visible label. The taste was probably despicable, but the satisfaction he got from it after emptying it made me jealous.

We stayed talking for many long hours. Later, our conversation shifted to the disaster topic. Egor's testimony could be useful to me for my report. He liked to talk about himself. He lived alone, as a recluse in the Zone, but his desire to capture attention was intact. I questioned him relentlessly. He told me about his wanderings, his discoveries. Egor seemed very well informed. Apparently, he had a close relative who was in the plant at the fatal moment. Kind of like me. He described the famous April 26th, 1986, to me as if he had been there himself.

'The employees were playing cards the night of the accident. It was very laid-back, nothing like it is now. Today, if a hammer falls on a staff member's toe, the whole country is aware of it and endless inspection procedures are launched. The plants are much better operated. I wouldn't go so far as to say that the risk is insignificant, but I mean, it's just like that.'

'Yes, certainly, but that does not prevent new accidents from occurring. Anyway, do Stalkers exist in Japan?' "

He swept the space with a wave of his hand.

'No ... well, what's the point... And it's not comparable with Ukraine. Nothing will ever be comparable with this place.'

He spoke these last words with seriousness I did not suspect him capable of. We left each other at this last remark, Egor returning to his lair and us to our slum. I tried to fall asleep.

I left the tent in the early morning. The dawn and its orange shades unfolded peacefully. I had a new curiosity to satisfy. I wanted to go to the hospital in Pripyat, the basement to be precise. I asked Andrei to arrange a visit together. He immediately accepted. The next day, we found ourselves in front of the building. He had a big smile on his face, rather proud to have seen me change my mind: 'After you, my friend!' he said, with a wink as unsettling as it was intriguing.

I entered the building, armed with a thousand precautions. *44 microsieverts.* The counter was pleading. Above my shoulder, I heard: 'stop that thing, it'll drive you crazy.' I took Andrei's advice and turned it off. We were now alone in the face of danger.

At the bottom of corridor 4 was an armoured door. No one really knew what was on the other side. The archival documents suggested sensitive medical equipment. Some speculated that there would be a secret reserve where poison and useful substances had been stored during the Cold War. A waste of time according to Andrei. The access key had been lost. The door was impassable, even with the most prodigious force. 'There's something more interesting, follow me,' he says.

I should have been terrified or excited, but I remained impassive. Basically, it was just another building, although a little more dangerous than the others. Garbage was littering the ground. The air was dirty and humid. Mould was eating away at some walls. We were progressing slowly, but without fear. Andrei was in conquered territory. He rejoiced to have me with him and to guide me into the dark depths of Pripyat.

We arrived in a small warehouse. Andrei lit up the room with his headlamp revealing rows of vials and utensils of all kinds. Some containers still held liquids in multicoloured shades. The labels were missing or unreadable. 'The bastards!' Andrei was angry. Apparently, individuals had stolen some. Objects from the Zone were sold on the Darknet and elsewhere. Some slightly disturbed collectors did not hesitate to spend countless amounts to make them their own and make themselves look interesting. But it wasn't just medical equipment. Clothes sat in piles. The fabrics were wrinkled, tangled.

In the next room was a mattress and a small re-frigerator. I laid my hand on the dusty handle. I was ready to open it, but at the last moment I stopped. Out of curiosi-ty, I turned on the Geiger counter again. *54 microsieverts.* Every second I spent here drastically increased my chances of developing cancer or worse.

I tried to call Andrei, but I couldn't. He had vaguely said something to me before he disappeared, I had already forgotten what. He was probably busy photographing the site and identifying anomalies. My concern was increasing. Alone, I didn't feel safe. In addition, I was suffering from a terrible headache, which made the situation suffocating. I felt a hand on my shoulder. Instinctively, I turned around and grabbed the man by the throat, ready to kill him. An-drei looked at me both surprised and smiling.

'Shall we go?' he asked.

'Yes, I want to get out of here.'

'I really thought you were gonna hit me, you know.'

'So did I. I'm on edge right now. I feel like the Zone is making me impulsive.'

'In that case, maybe it's time for you to leave it.'

These last words left me pensive. Should I put an end to my wanderings? How could I be convinced to leave the exclusion zone and what would I do once I'd left? My life would be bland, the stakes flat and futile.

The Zone had attracted me to it and now kept me in it. Like a spider, it had woven its web, trapping my reason and judgement. I was captive and aware of it. Paradoxical-ly, the Zone had also liberated me by satisfying the question of my identity and the existential quest that had been luring me since childhood.

I didn't want to run away. There was still so much to discover. I decided to stay a little bit longer.

Chapter 5 — Cataract

15 h 34.

The sun was high in the sky, the wind remained calm. A very slight mist emanated from the forest. The conditions were ideal.

My GPS indicated the route to Pripyat. I carefully followed the path until I spotted the junction I was waiting for. I had to weave between swamps and then take the small pathway that went towards the trees. It was there. I had finally reached the entrance to the Red Forest. Ecstatic, I meticulously parked my car and then set off on the track.

The path was dark, dotted with deformed shrubs and disturbing plant structures. Many signs indicated the radioactive hazard. They lined the path like amulets, trying to alert the visitor to the danger waiting for him. It would take more than that to talk me out of it.

Although unaware of my destination, I walked with great strides, swift and impatient, determined to penetrate the impenetrable. I rushed through the trees, letting the forest suck me in. I wanted to reach its core, to sink deeper and deeper into its very heart.

The woods surrounded me, they seemed to be watching my progress. A seductive fragrance came out of it and disturbed my senses. This aromatic distraction almost made me forget the radiation. The meter was starting to panic. I looked around.

18 microsieverts.

It was still reasonable. I didn't care, I continued on my way. My mind was a little foggy, detached from my usual concerns. Arriving at another junction, I turned left in a completely random manner. I was particularly fond of the idea of letting myself be guided by my steps. I did not want to plan a direction or follow a path but instead, I wanted to trust my instincts, the ones that rarely betrayed me.

My journey was sometimes arduous. Often I felt compelled to overcome certain obstacles. In particular, I was forced to cross a frozen river. The undertaking was dangerous and, since the ice was breaking in some places, I had to be skilful. However, I ignored my soaked feet and persevered in my progress.

It was snowing very hard, but the sky was clear, almost immaculate. The sound of the meter did not fade.

24 microsieverts.

I didn't care and doubled my effort, driven by an intense shiver of excitement. My breathing was accelerating. I wanted to push the limits, to extend my progress to the ends of this forest.

Nevertheless, I was forced to stop.

Obviously, I had come to a dead end. The path seemed to disappear into what looked like a tiny cemetery. A handful of graves lay there, dilapidated and partially buried. They were arranged in a disorderly manner, as if they had been built in haste and without any desire for coherence.

No names, inscriptions or religious symbols were displayed. The layout was irregular and seemed confusing. The graves looked menacing, but they didn't frighten me. I went around them, looking for traces of a trail at the foot of the trees.

I wanted to sneak through the forest, wander beyond. I noticed a rift between bushes, a path seemed to be emerging. I ignored the spiky brambles and committed myself to pushing through them. Shrubs blocked my way, but I didn't care. Little reddish thorns challenged me, but I ignored them.

Something was arousing my curiosity. I thought I could distinguish a sound in the background. A mysterious metallic buzzing was floating on the air towards me. Maybe it was the wind that mixed with the whining of the meter? Maybe the noise was made by a machine or an animal?

My ears were straining, trying to identify this sound which was lingering threateningly on the air. It was gaining on me. A sibylline whine trapped in its own mysterious frequency. I was falling into a trance. I looked around, considering the idea of turning back. However, I was unable to: the forest called to me, its aura was irresistible. I had no choice. I had to continue at all costs.

I made the decision to crawl under a tangle of brambles. I kept moving forward. My steps were now energetic and hurried, I was doped by senseless excitement. The meter was screaming relentlessly, becoming almost unbearable.

38 microsieverts.

I was stubborn and determined. The vegetation was confusing. It was not abnormal in itself, but it seemed to be imbued with the same floating sensation which was inside of me. It was invasive without being suffocating.

I finally arrived in a small glade, delimited by thick bushes and branches of unreal dimensions.

The air was filled with fragrances, as seductive as they were mysterious. Time seemed to have been altered. On the ground, the roots of the trees were very visible and intertwined in an almost sacral disorder. I had an ambiguous feeling, a state divided between fulfilment and misunderstanding. Even though I had reached its heart, the forest seemed more elusive to me than ever before. I still didn't know what I was looking for. A sensational feeling? The enjoyment of the broken taboo? Various thoughts absorbed me.

56 microsieverts.

I was gradually losing consciousness of my wooded environment, my mind was going astray. It was lost in idyllic dreams. A big hare crossed right in front of me. It was alone and paid no attention to me. My eyes followed it with a blissful look as if they were distinguishing this kind of animal for the first time. I could have spent hours wandering through the woods, captivated by this bewitching and bucolic atmosphere.

66 microsieverts.

Obscure introspections attacked me. The wind had slackened, nature had fallen into a shattering silence. The cold was almost imperceptible. It was as if I were wrapped in an exquisite dream, a soft, infinite cocoon. A delicious nonchalance had set in. The air was soft. I felt light, indifferent. The forest had taken possession of me. Consenting, I closed my eyes to let myself be caught by this misty monster.

***

74 microsieverts.

The squeaks of the meter eventually brought me to my senses. Two hours had passed since I entered this forest and deep snow had begun to fall.

Without hesitation, I turned back, walking at full speed in order to precede the night that was coming. I tried to retrace my steps from earlier, the traces would still be present, preserved by the powder snow.

At the junctions, I knew exactly which directions to take. The trajectory was still fresh in my mind. However, some details seemed to me to be new, such as an embankment marked by an indecipherable sign or a stream which seemed much wider than before. Anyway, I probably hadn't payed enough attention the first time.

As I walked on, I began to notice that the snow had removed the oldest traces. Unbothered, I decided to follow my intuition. About thirty minutes passed. The light gradually dimmed and I was still having increasing difficulty identifying the footprints. I remained calm, convinced of the goodwill of this forest.

I finally found the frozen river I had crossed: no remnants of broken ice, the surface was smooth and unaltered. There was no evidence of my previous visit. This was not surprising, the cold had probably intensified a lot during my walk. The water had solidified again, understandably. Not overly concerned, I crossed calmly. My movements were methodical, the ice would not give way. I felt confident and easily reached the opposite shore.

The atmosphere had changed somewhat, but the forest was still as bewitching as ever. A few more meters and I would reach the edge of the woods. I rushed, a little reassured at having avoided a tragedy. My vehicle was not far away. Only a few more seconds and I would be there. It must have been near the big tree right next to the log. Or rather near the birch tree that bordered the river. Well, no, it must have been on a shoulder further south. Yes, that must have been it, I had probably parked it discreetly to avoid attention.

The light faded as the darkness of the winter night descended. I was shivering. The cold was biting and gusts were starting to blow. I needed a shelter. The impermeability of my gloves seemed to diminish, I could feel the frostbite eating at my fingers more and more. I rubbed my hands vigorously, pressing them against my chest. It was a survival technique I had learned on television. However, my defences were weakening. My face was lacerated by ever more powerful icy gusts. I took a circular and distraught look at it. I felt like prey hunted by an imperceptible, but omnipresent enemy. I gathered my courage and started thinking rapidly. The landscape seemed identical to my memories, yet it was not the right place.

I swore loud and clear: '*Kurva!*'.

The poison of doubt was spreading in me. The screams of the counter did not help my concentration. I remembered Andrei's warnings. 'No one will pick you up there.' My unease was growing and I had no desire to spend the night in this forest. I didn't want to do it because the prospect of the nightmares I would have out here terrified me so much. I shouted for help, begging with all my strength. The echo of my voice slapped my face. I shouted louder, burning my lungs with the monstrous effort. My pleas remained unheard. With my hands in front of the visor to protect myself, I tried at all costs to move forward, to survive a little longer. Stumbling and out of breath, I was forced to slow down. My sight was blurred, my senses were diminished. Exhaustion was catching up with me. Slowly, the darkness enveloped me.

A powerful heaviness inhabited my body. My limbs seemed inert and uncontrollable. I wasn't dead. My conscience suggested thoughts to me. I still had a survival instinct. I felt that strong hands were grabbing me and I was leaving the ground. I could feel the change in gravity that was happening and the caresses of the wind on my face. I was trying to understand, to interpret these sensations.

Oleksandr carried me on his back in a rather primitive way, a bit like carrying a bag of rice up a hill.

Was he my saviour? How did he find me? I was unable to say or to understand anything.

'You look very pale,' he said, looking amused.

Oleksandr seemed much more animated than usual. Was he bipolar? I had never seen him smile before. It had taken my near death to see him display a positive emotion. He was perplexing, but almost endearing. The bugger seemed almost satisfied to find me in this state.

He took me to his vehicle and placed me in the back while dressing me in a survival blanket. Oleksandr sat at the front whistling and started the 4 × 4. I struggled to keep my eyelids open and keep a visual record of what was happening. The heating and fatigue got the better of me. I fell asleep in a few seconds.

When I woke up, I instantly understood that I was no longer in the Zone. Something had changed. Something perceptible and striking enough for me to notice immediately. A glance through the window was sufficient to convince me. The sky was different, devoid of the hues of the Zone. I was watching the room around me. It was Oleksandr's place. He brought me back with him to the suburbs of Kiev. It seemed unreal to me to find myself in his house, his character was so enigmatic and his secrets so inviolable.

I had slept for about 11 hours. He gave me some vitamin pills and served me a wonderfully strong coffee.

'Sorry, I don't have anything else. You'll have to make do with it. It'll get you back on your feet. I don't know how much radiation you exposed yourself to but it must have been pretty gigantic. What the hell did you go there for?'

'Actually, I have no idea. I felt extremely attracted to this forest. It was as if a singular force was whispering to me to go there. I lost all reasoning, all coherence of mind and I entered it. I went head first and ventured deeper and deeper. I didn't understand what was going on. I don't think I'm the first one to go there.'

'Oh, no, don't worry about it! Others made that mistake before you. Some have even camped there already. But you should know that walking through it alone in winter and not telling anyone is foolish. '

'Andrei was aware of my intention', I replied.

'That doesn't mean he would have gone to get you. You know, I've heard some pretty sordid stories about this forest. Some young people nearly died there a few years ago. They were practicing some kind of ritual for one of their birthdays. We don't know what really happened, but only one of them came back. He refused to speak and was placed in a psychiatric hospital. All this to tell you that visiting that place is not insignificant.'

I thought that the Zone was indeed a victim of its success. I was thinking about the two teenage skinheads. Like them, there must have been hundreds of people coming to ransack the place and have fun. Their behaviour was becoming more and more aggressive. Their immature escapades were dangerous. I asked Oleksandr about them. Faithful to himself, he shrugged his shoulders and sighed.

'They are stupider than they are fearsome. I've already met a few of them. The most harmful are those who venture out alone. Almost all of them are armed. In fact, even some ordinary visitors are. Once I led a group of tourists and things got out of hand. At the time, the circuits were much freer. I took them wherever I wanted. The government had no control over anything, I had carte blanche. So I guided them to a fairly isolated and well-preserved area. They were quite excited, they felt like pioneers and thought of themselves as such. Some had drunk a few beers and others were under the influence of marijuana. In the afternoon, two fools provoked a Dutch tourist by pretending to push him into the Pripyat River. He didn't like it at all. A brawl broke out and one of them drew a knife. The guy ended up in the ER with five stitches, but the case was hushed up.'

'Is that why you stopped the visits? Did you get fired?'

'No. I left of my own free will a few months later. I told you before, I'm no longer interested in the Zone as such.'

I tried to get back on track.

'When were the first visits made?'

'With guides?'

'Yes,' I replied.

'All this merry mess started in the late '90s. At the time, nothing was regulated and the Zone was infinitely more dangerous than it is today. Visitors and Stalkers behaved in any way they liked: they drank river water and lit campfires.

As I told you, some of them went about at night in gangs and took ill-considered risks. Thank God, the situation has changed a little. Subsequently, the government has more or less secured things by institutionalising visits with agencies approved by the state services. Things accelerated in the early 2000s and especially after the Orange Revolution. Now with the new sarcophagus, it's much less dangerous, so it's even easier. The popularity of the exclusion zone is exponential. Tourism is going to explode. In a few years, the Zone will compete with Disneyland, you'll see.'

He seemed disillusioned and took up the serious look to which he had accustomed me:

'You can't stay here very long. Where do you want me to drop you off?'

'I'll walk back, I'll be fine. I will use public transport.'

Unsurprisingly, Oleksandr nodded. Without saying a word, he put a few coins in my pocket and pushed me out. Not without some difficulty, I found the bus stop stuck between two blocks of quite hideous buildings.

I arrived at my hotel after what seemed like an endless journey. Some snot-nosed kids had passed by and played animal noises on their phones to distract the driver.

Readapting to an urban environment was confusing after living in the Zone for a while. The car horns, the music in the shops, the discussions of passers-by in the street... All these noises annoyed me. All these people in motion were polluting my field of vision. Bright fast-food chains were aggressive to the eye. Maidan square still had the scars of the 2014 uprisings. References to free Ukraine and the European Union were scattered throughout the city.

In Kiev, the average income was 250 euros while corruption was at its highest. Ukraine's GDP was now five times lower than its Polish neighbour, though they had once been equal. I was thinking about that damn report I was supposed to write. What exactly had I promised my supervisor? I was no longer totally sure. I finally arrived at my destination. My hotel room seemed dull, soulless to me. The radiator was broken and the insulation almost non-existent. I wanted to escape as soon as possible. One more night and I would leave this place.

Before going to sleep, I took a Scottish shower. The icy water flowed over me like a saving lotion, invigorating everything in its path. I felt reborn, a new being would return to the Zone.

I came out of the bathroom to grab the only bottle of alcohol in the minibar and kneel on my bed. The liquid was infective, but I remained impassive and determined to empty it to the last drop. I end up falling asleep, my mind spinning and my heart soothed.

In the early morning, I left the hotel a little haggard and started wandering in the street. The alleys were deserted, Kiev was still drowsy. Only a few solitary taxis were roaming along the capital's main arteries. One of them stopped. I quickly got inside and handed a piece of paper to the driver. The GPS coordinates had been scribbled in a hurry. He frowned and then started the car. The taxi leapt forward in a cloud of black smoke.

Second Part

The blizzard was exhilarating. I could have sworn that two unmoving eyes were staring at me through the branches. I felt watched. Something was listening to me, looking at me. The forest was dark and cold. The shadows were intimidating and threatening. The moon also seemed troubling. It emitted a weak glow, just enough for me to be able to distinguish the silhouette from the trees. The thing was following me. It seemed to have an extraordinary agility as it was so discreet and undetectable. I felt its presence while ignoring the nature of its existence. I would have liked to annihilate it, destroy it by an outpouring of violence. However, I was getting used to it, as when we tolerate an enemy too weak to act. That's how I tried to tame my fear. After all, maybe it was harmless. Probably my sharp mind was falling into a disproportionate psychosis. My vision was warped. The colours seemed distorted to me. The blue tones were unreal. The contrasts, on the other hand, were very strong, almost aggressive. I was trying to stay calm. I was struggling to breathe. But already, it was coming back, quicker and quicker. The blizzard was roaring.

Chapter 6 — Intent

8th day in the Zone.

Amanda was a fearless and rather clever girl. She seemed to be one step ahead of the other Stalkers. Her beautiful emerald eyes shone in the night. They betrayed a kindness, but also an unlimited curiosity, which immediately made people feel comfortable and softened their behaviour.

I met Amanda on a full moon evening on the roof of the cultural centre. Andrei had introduced her to me with enthusiasm. The two seemed to be linked by a discreet complicity, a friendship of quite an unusual nature., We chatted for hours together, lit by a small, rather modest candle that warmed our hands. We got to the point very quickly. Amanda was looking for the treasure. She had already roamed the Zone on multiple occasions, but had not made significant progress so far. I suggested that we could work together, coordinate our efforts. She nodded with a smile.

Andrei seemed disinterested in the loot, but listened carefully. He opined, interjected, issuing more or less relevant opinions. His words were few and far between, but welcomed. He acted like a wise man with advice for his disciples. Amanda wanted to explore further into the woodlands bordering the exclusion zone, including those adjacent to Belarus. These areas were rather ignored by the maps and various existing plans due to the lack of in-frastructure present. For my part, I was betting on the northeast part, where a few abandoned buildings were located.

'And Duga, have you thought about that?' I asked.

'The perimeter is quite well guarded, it's difficult to get in without a group of tourists,' said Amanda. 'A guard is constantly positioned with a dog.'

She turned to me with an interrogating look on her face.

'Maybe you could go there?'

'I'll make a trip, I've read a lot about it. Perhaps I can find something new.'

'Perfect,' Andrei added. 'I could brief you on Duga, I've done the ascent several times.'

'Is Oleksandr aware of all this?'

The other two exchanged a brief look, I could have sworn they looked embarrassed.

Andrei dodged quickly:

'I don't know, but let's not involve him in our research, he'll slow us down. And it's been so long since I've seen him... Well! It's late now. I propose that you meet us here in two days.'

Andrei extinguished the candle with his hands. Despite the polar temperatures, we decided to sleep on the roof. Waking up there would be splendid and the heavenly canopy would watch over us. The silence of the place was only disturbed by the rustling wind and Andrei's sporadic coughing. Before I fell asleep, I took a few pictures of the sky. The stars shone in a sumptuous ballet whose choreography was as calculated as it was mysterious.

That night I experienced new, hyper-realistic and frightening dreams. I could see myself running through the Zone, chased by a horde of dogs, bloody lips and sharp fangs. Their radioactive bites infected my body with rabies and all kinds of horrible diseases. I was faster than them. I rushed through the forest at a mad pace, slaloming between the shrubs, leaping above the brambles. The wind carried the dogs' howling, encouraging me to accelerate even more. I gained speed, my maneuvers on the ground became more vigorous, my balance more fragile. I stumbled. My body was propelled to the ground in a cloud of black dust. The sun irradiated me with its hot rays while scratches caused me burning pain. It only took about ten seconds for the dogs to catch up with me. They all barked louder than each other. I could distinguish the rage that emanated from their eyes, the murderous instinct that animated them. I raised one last glance to the sky, the prodigious zenith that was before me. The heat of the summer was suffocating. The solar star would observe my death, and perhaps, alleviate it? I didn't have time to think any more. A fierce scream rang out and the fangs fell wildly.

Despite my nightmare, I woke up peacefully. A new exciting day was coming up. Andrei had gone to take care of 'some personal business' and I found myself alone in the forest with Amanda. She moved like a cat. She tamed her environment with disconcerting ease while I struggled to avoid thorns and peat bogs. Amanda laughed at my wobbly gait. I felt almost ashamed. To reassure myself, I looked for her weaknesses.

She finally started the conversation.

'I reread the press clippings, I listened to the broadcasts. During the Chernobyl disaster, the media and experts from Western Europe announced that the territory would be uninhabitable for 20,000 years. Today the Ukrainian government has committed itself to cleaning up the Zone by 2065. Some say it's impossible. Who to believe? How do you fight an invisible enemy and ensure its total eradication?'

'We will never succeed in doing so completely, I have no illusions about that!'

'It seems that new threats are emerging,' she continued. 'The Zone is now the scene of cyber attacks driven by who knows who. It's just another invisible enemy, but this one is being deliberately directed. I hope they will identify those responsible...'

'Did you keep up with the legal procedure that followed the disaster?'

'Of course! Among others, the accused were Viktor Bryukhanov, head of the plant, Nikolai Fomin, the chief engineer, Anatoly Dyatlov, an assistant engineer and Yuri Laushkin, inspector of the Nuclear Supervisory Committee to the Soviet Union. After a year and a half of proceedings, Bryukhanov was found guilty of the accident. A 10-year prison sentence was requested against him and Dyatlov. Dyatlov and Fomin were also accused of conducting experiments on the reactor without the necessary permits.

During the tests, the reactor power was reduced to 700 MW and the automatic shutdown systems were deactivated. No coordination with the reactor designer and responsible scientists had taken place. From the rest of the hearings, it emerged that the plant staff were insufficiently trained and did not have all the necessary knowledge to perform their role. Nikolai Fomin was less fortunate than the others. According to some witnesses, he tried to end his life a few days before the trial. Though he was properly convicted like the others, he was diagnosed with serious disorders and doctors declared him unfit to serve his sentence. Instead, he was transferred to a psychiatric hospital where he was treated for some time before leaving. It seems that he finished his career at the Kalinin nuclear power plant...'

I remained silent through her monologue. She continued:

'You know, I travelled a lot before I moved to Cologne. I have walked the deserts of Kazakhstan and the steppes of Siberia. My family had a house on the banks of the Karelia River. It was in Russia that I met Andrei, he was camping on the heights, near my native village. We lost sight of each other for a few years, but our common interest in the Zone brought us together. Where are you staying in Kiev?'

'In a seedy hotel whose name I forgot.'

She smiled, my memory problems amused her.

'How long have you had this?'

'This?'

'This amnesia.'

I was irritated when she suggested this deficiency.

'I don't have amnesia. The cold and lack of sleep affect my thought process. This environment is of such sensory intensity, how can we not be affected?'

'Um, I'm doing pretty well. Andrei suffers from some side effects, mainly nausea or vomiting. He spends too much time here. I advised him to go to a specialist, but he doesn't see the point. He says he's careful, he knows the Zone well now, but I guess the radiation still affects him. We had to warn you, no one leaves here unscathed. That's why the Babushkas chose to stay.' She paused for a moment before questioning me: 'Still... I'm curious. What kinds of memories do you have from your childhood here? Do you have any flashbacks?'

'It's quite confusing. I remember the look of the trees that bordered the entrance to the city, but also the wallpaper in my room. On the other hand, I have difficulty visualising what our daily life was like and how it affected me. It is said that the environment of our childhood affects our entire existence. I was shaped by this place, somehow I belong to it.'

'Will you bring your children here?'

'Probably not. I wouldn't want them to be haunted by any past, whatever it may be.'

She suddenly changed the subject.

'So you're a journalist?'

'Yes, I work in a small publication. We do reports, miscellaneous facts without much pretension, sometimes a little politics.'

'I see… Can I read your article when it's finished?'

'Actually, I still don't know what to write about. I was thinking of doing a subject on the tourist development of the Zone, but that type of reporting already exists by the dozen.'

'Why don't you tell your own story? A former resident of Pripyat who became Stalker, it could be very exciting.'

'It would be better as a novel, but I have no literary ambition.'

She took a long breath.

'Who first mentioned the treasure of Pripyat to you? What did they tell you?'

I had a moment's pause. A slow frenzy was taking hold of me. It was more than just a common headache, more of a dizziness, with a feeling of déjà vu that made me uncomfortable. Was I aware of anything? Of course I was, but I was unable to expose that memory. I only recalled murmurs that suggested clues that I couldn't decipher. It was an opaque, elusive feeling. Doubt was germinating in me, spreading its horrors throughout my whole body.

***

2 days later.

I was back with Amanda.

'What's up? Have you been able to make any progress?'

'Not really. I went to see Duga. I climbed it to the top. It was beautiful, but I didn't find anything.'

'Didn't you meet anyone there?'

'No! Not a clue, nothing.'

'Are you sure about that?'

'Absolutely.'

She seemed sceptical.

'So too bad for Duga. You should try to get to know the man who lives in the northern part of the Zone. We call him The Howler. I saw him once, it was a few months ago. They say he goes out a lot more in winter. Maybe you'll have a chance with him.'

'Isn't he dangerous?'

'No, not at all. He's a good man, but he can be unpredictable. Don't persist if he's having a bad day.'

'How can I reach him?'

She laughed.

'I think he'll find you first. All you have to do is get lost across the river to the northeast. Go off the trails and follow the horizon. Maybe he'll tell you something. He can be very talkative, depending on the situation. By the way, you didn't tell me how you got into the Zone for the first time.'

'I'm here because of Oleksandr. I couldn't have got in without him. Besides, you and Andrei seem to know him well, don't you? What do you think of him?'

Amanda was silent. She seemed hesitant, almost intimidated. She was uncomfortable at the mention of him. She bit her lip.

'I shouldn't say this, but he scares me. I don't trust him. He's kind of an enigmatic person, you know. Andrei is the one who often sees him, but he fears him. He even forbade me to be alone with him. Not that he's dangerous... It's just ... well ... he's like that. We owe him a lot.'

'Why?'

She bit her lip again, this time until she bled.

'Oh nothing, some old stories... Oleksandr is a good person. He had a difficult life, that's all. That must explain his mood swings.'

She didn't seem to want to say anything more.

'Tell me again about Duga, did Andrei go back?'

'I think he goes from time to time. He has doubts about the solidity of the structure. Didn't he explain it to you? It is more than 30 years old and has not been maintained for ages. But the sunsets are beautiful, they say. What is your next goal?'

'You know, sometimes I think about giving up and leaving.'

'Don't do that. Don't do that.'

The tone of her voice had suddenly changed. Amanda seemed almost threatening to me.

'I mean, that would be a shame. We make a good team. I'm sure we'll get what we want. We're making progress every day.'

I remained silent. In the face of my apparent scepticism, she stopped and pressed my arm. She stared at me and said only one word.

'Stay.'

The magnetism of her gaze had enough to be persuasive. It pierced my defences, charmed me as much as it frightened me.

We arrived near a glade where some houses seemed to have remained away from the villages. It was an old farmhouse with a barn and a few silos. We went around the small courtyard at the front of the house. There were still some gardening tools sitting about. I had the feeling that the departure of the occupants had been very recent. The interior was clean and seemed to be well maintained. Bread was sitting out in the kitchen as if someone would arrive any minute to cut it up. Barely dusty newspapers were stacked on the ground. Amanda broke the silence: 'I think I knew her. This Babushka died a short time ago.'

She didn't seem particularly touched. The tone of her voice betrayed a certain detachment. Perhaps she had been expecting this discovery?

We were entering the second room. The bedroom was tiny and had no furniture, except for a single bed in very poor condition. The mattress was quite thick, but pretty rustic. The patterns were discoloured and almost imperceptible. I realised that I had missed a detail. A note was stuck to the door. It mentioned Kopatchi. It was a small village located west of the Pripyat River. After the evacuations, the decision was made to bury the houses in order to avoid returns and deter looters. They were now buried under clay mounds and radioactive hazard warning signs. Very few buildings had escaped this fate. The Kindergarten was one of them. It had therefore not been spared from looting. Wrongdoers were bound to come here and steal things or ransack the place.

I examined the note. It must have been hung recently. The writing was blurry and hasty. It could have been mine. I tore off the piece of paper and buried it in my pocket. I didn't know what to do with it, but my instinct was to keep it safe.

Amanda put her head in her arms : 'I'm tired, let's go back to Pripyat.'

***

The darkness was descending, permeating the landscape, flooding the most remote areas with shadows and blackness. I decided to go up to the roof of the building. The night was cool and dotted with opal-coloured stars. I smoked a cigarette, observing the constellations and the heavens. These bright stars were perfectly visible due to the absence of light pollution and other urban distractions. It is said that at certain times you could even see Saturn. I was trying to distinguish what my imagination was whispering at me. The smoke from my cigarette was rising in the sky towards the distant stars. My gaze was lost in this cosmic enigma, where deep secrets seemed to be buried. I thought that each luminous star represented as many truths as one would have to grasp and clash to obtain an answer to the existential questions that pulled me. I was thinking about the future, the anguish that was coming.

My eyes were drawn to a movement: a silhouette came to join me on the roof. She sat cross-legged in front of me. Amanda had tears slowly running down her face. They seemed almost too clear. Were they false?

'Are you not asleep?' I asked.

'Impossible. I don't intend to,' she replied. 'Insomnia strikes me as much as you.'

'You know, sometimes I wonder. If I leave this place, will I be able to come back?'

'Of course, you've already done it.'

'What do you mean?' I exclaimed in a hostile voice.

'You really don't remember anything?' She whispered as she sobbed.

I remained silent, my eyes dark.

'You came here eight months ago …'

'What are you talking about?!' I shouted.

'That is the truth. You know the Zone as well as we do. You know that deep down inside. You just forgot about it…'

'That's enough! That's enough! I don't trust you anymore. You're messing with my brain, you're even worse than the other two.' '

She took my hand and pressed it vigorously against hers.

'Please …'

Her gaze was both enticing and despicable. I could have kissed her as much as killed her right now. I pushed her away violently. She fell heavily to the ground, her face covered with tears.

'Get out of here! I don't need you anymore.'

Indifferent to my protests, she stood up and grabbed hold of me more desperately, her cries redoubling in intensity.

'Please don't go, please.'

I freed my hands and with even more unbridled brutality, I pushed her again, hard. She was on the edge of the roof, only a thin cornice separated her from the drop. Her eyes were swollen with despair. I turned my back on her and went down the ladder that led to the ground.

Should I believe her? Was she trustworthy? I clenched my teeth, shaking with rage. No, she was exactly like the others, manipulative and driven by her own interests. From the beginning she had been playing me. I was more and more convinced of it, her gentle features concealed a pernicious being. May she rot in hell! I wished her death. As for me, I would continue on my way, my fists clenched and my heart full of anger.

I couldn't tell know how much time had gone by. I was possessed by a throbbing vertigo. The trees seemed identical, but the horizon, yes, the horizon seemed clearer. The cold was less biting while the wind was almost conciliatory. But I wasn't crazy, it was still snowing. I could see the snowflakes falling. Were they real? I hurriedly grabbed them with my hands and touched them to my face as if to convince myself of their existence. The effect was chilling. Yes, I was experiencing these sensations well. The icy crystals melted, dripping on my cheeks, and I cried with joy. I wasn't mad. Winter had not gone, I had only been in the exclusion zone for a few days. I was always the same, clairvoyant and intrepid. I had been lied to. The villains. Of course they lied to me. I dreamed of twisting their necks, nailing their faces and hanging their carcasses in the Red Forest. Yes, that's what they deserved. As these violent thoughts poured into me, I felt the usual pain: the recurring and unbearable headache that constantly returned. I felt that someone, something was drumming against my brain, like a door being pushed down with a battering ram. The pain made me sweat and pant. I pressed my skull frantically into the frozen ground, desperate for an escape from this ordeal, for a more suitable end. The cold was real. The horizon had darkened. The blizzard's howl was about to resound. I closed my eyes as if blinding myself would hide my pain and repel the nightmare that was spreading inside me. Winter had never dispersed. It had maintained itself, inflexible, as if persuaded to defeat me. I thought it had succeeded. I planned to surrender, stop this excess suffering and put an end to the anxiety. I no longer really knew who I was, what shaped me and what pushed me to act. I felt deprived of my conscience. My ego was gone. My past existence had been annihilated. I had become a near-human. A naked being, empty of substance and reduced to a wandering entitywhose end could not be anything other than a painful death. Tears were flowing. A fragment of humanity was still sleeping in me. My liquid tears were warm and drowned my eyes as if to purify me from my suffering. I had to run away. An inner voice was whispering at me to disappear. The idea was as devious as its author. It had invaded me like a torrent, carrying everything in its path, until it reached me in the depths of my heart. I was trying to resist that intention, that temptation. The dilemma was tenacious, I couldn't stand this confrontation anymore.

Chapter 7 — Fracas

10th day in the Zone.

An owl was hooting. I unfolded the tent near an imposing conifer, preparing myself to spend yet another night in the Zone. I had somewhat lost track of the hours as if my perception of time had been affected by radioactivity. It was impossible for me to sleep. Slumber was toying with me. Sneakily, Morpheus attracted me and then moved away enough to keep me frustrated and awake.

To keep myself busy, I decided to watch the videotapes of the camera we had placed with Andrei. I was curious about what the images could reveal. I had the recording of the last two days unfolded in chronological order.

I was a little unsettled to see myself under the effect of a thermal representation so much it made me look like an intruder. On the screen, Andrei and I could be seen walking around in the buggy garage, hiding the device before we retired. Then it was nothingness. As the hours passed, no movement was taking shape. The room was empty. I accelerated the scrolling. Still nothing. There was only the last day of registration corresponding to today. Finally, at 6:00 p.m. the image came to life. A silhouette appeared in the camera field. My pulse rushed. I immediately switched back to real speed. The individual moved quickly and precisely. Obviously, he had broken in here before and had his bearings. The man seemed tall and strong, but was unrecognisable. It was just a cluster of purple colours and yellow tones. He hadn't come alone. A second person accompanied him, much more ill at ease and with softer, less confident movements. A projector had been turned on and placed on the side. The thermal camera was glitching. Coloured slicks merged into a psychedelic mixture. With the room now lit, I was afraid that the camera would not be sufficiently hidden.

The two men stayed for more than an hour. They seemed to have come only to talk sothey didn't interact with the room. One of them, the tall one, seemed to be holding a notepad. He wrote and drew frantically, pointing things out to his sidekick. Then it was his turn to express himself. The first one had his hands on his hips and walked a hundred paces listening to him. His body language betrayed a clear domination in his relationship with the second individual. The latter seemed more obedient than co-operative. Paradoxically, he seemed calmer as if he had a greater distance from their situation, from the problem that occupied their debate. I cursed myself for not having the sound. I was intrigued by their conversation. What was the justification for a clandestine meeting in this hard-to-reach building? Why did the tall one seems so tense, so anxious? Finally, the discussion stopped. The fellow repacked the projector while the second one stuffed the notepad into a bag. The two individuals escaped from the room. The colours disappeared and the video became monotonous again. I turned off my phone.

The night was troubled. I must say that my sub-conscious was fertile. Fantastic spectra and visions followed one another without any coherence. My tormented sleep was abruptly broken by a crashing noise. Worried, I woke up with a start, my senses alert and my forehead soaked in sweat. The nocturnal calm contrasted with my agitation.

Had I heard a shot?

I had the greatest difficulty distinguishing dream from reality. My imagination had been so stimulated recently that my mind had turned into a double-edged sword. It was playing tricks on me, hurting me and shattering my perception of reality.

Had I really heard that scream?

I remembered Andrei's story and his attack outside the Jupiter factory. My skin was oozing fear. My camp was exposed, visible to anyone who approached it without even looking for it. I was trapped. Instinctively, I grabbed my knife. It was a meagre defence for the terror that animated me. Outside, the wind was roaring, making the branches and fasteners of my tent squeak.

Was I alone in this forest?

It was not the wolves that frightened me, but human beings. Despite the cold, I was sweating heavily, trying to make a decision as best I could. Tired of my passive tension, I silently stepped out of the tent, looking for explanations.

The night was clear. The moon was shining brightly enough to distinguish through the trees.

I slipped between the bushes, always on the alert and as discreet as possible. The air was humid and full of odours.

A branch cracked. On the lookout, I suddenly stopped all movement. I was trying to imagine an explanation. It could have been the wind or an animal. Maybe it was a soldier? Maybe it was Stalkers? There had only been one shot, with no apparent retaliation. My watch indicated two o'clock in the morning. How long had it been since the shooting? Had it really been followed by a scream or was it the result of a crazy imagination? I remembered Andrei and the gun grip sticking out of his pants. The mobile network was inaccessible, it was impossible to contact him. I had to rely on myself.

The freezing night disturbed my thoughts. I didn't know what to do, taking a look around. Worried and frigid, I finally returned to the tent. I came back with more questions than answers. As natural sleep was now impossible to access, I swallowed a small magic tablet that I had stocked up on. This time, there would be no dreams but only the promise of a peaceful night. Not even the reactor blowout would wake me up.

**

The forest was dense and deep. The wind swirled the last dead leaves. I was lost in complex thoughts whose elusive ideas swirled in the air like eagles flying over their prey. I felt taunted by my own unconscious. It was a frustrating feeling of which I was the victim. A trap set by my mind for myself. I needed to put an end to this state of floating, to understand what was confronting me so determinedly. I could have remained absorbed in my dreams for thousands of years.

I stopped suddenly. My gaze had been captured by a curious object. Something was lying in the distance. An emerald cloth contrasted with the lightness of the snow. I slowly approached between hesitation and interest. No doubt about it, it was a corpse. Despite having no medical knowledge, I was wondering about the time of death. My common sense suggested that the last breath came only a few hours ago. The body was spread symmetrically as if the individual had fallen asleep peacefully. It looked like a mysterious totem pole with its frozen expression and its arms carefully unfolded, almost as a welcome sign.

It took me a few minutes to register the grace of its features, the softness of its cheekbones. I had been misled by the short hair and manly shoes, to say the least. The evidence of her femininity froze my blood. Strangely enough, the fact that it was a woman made me much more anxious than before.   Had she killed herself? Had she been murdered? What motive could justify such an act in such a place?

There was no evidence of any apparent injury, her physical integrity was intact. It could not have been the work of an animal that would have attacked her. The crime, if there was one, seemed perfectly executed. I wondered if she had suffered. Not that I had any empathy. I felt more intrigued than compassionate.

I rolled the body on its side, as gently as possible. I had never buried anyone with my own hands before. The body was heavy and difficult to handle. Maybe it was due to my fingers shaking nervously.

I started digging snow, frantically shaking my arms to scatter the different pine cones that were complicating my work. When the cavity was satisfactory, I carefully placed the corpse, smoothing down a lock of her hair which was twirling in the wind. I had already taken off her shoes and gloves. They would be more useful to me than to her. Slowly, almost religiously, I covered her body with snow. I made gentle movements as if they were likely to create pain, to damage the deceased. When my dark task was finished, I knelt down in front of the small mound of snow. I hadn't found any identity papers, any clues about this woman's life. No tattoos, no inscriptions. Not even a phone.

I walked away fast, but not thoughtlessly. The buried body was an enigma, an image that would haunt me forever. I hesitated to contact Andrei to tell him about my find. Maybe he was involved? I started to doubt it. As a precaution, I decided to keep the secret of my discovery. I finally chose to turn back, with a tormented mind and uncertain motivations. Uncomfortable, I tried to purge my thoughts, to turn my attention back to other things as if I was trying to minimise what I had witnessed. However, as I walked, I couldn't help but remember what I had seen, trying to solve the mystery of the victim. Was the body arranged for me to find it?

My paranoia was getting worse. I imagined myself observed and stalked. It was impossible for me to move forward without taking a quick look behind me. I felt so tiny in that snow-covered forest.

The fog was slowly rising in the sky. It dissipated as if to expose my position to some aerial spectator. The trees seemed taller and more numerous than ever. I was on the lookout, anticipating a possible attack. With one firm hand, I squeezed the grip of the knife in my jacket. I was ready to face anything. At least, I was trying to convince myself of that.

While I was thinking, I looked up at the treetops, trying to find a solution. My eyes were drawn to a peculiar object: something was levitating up there.   A shiver of fear crossed my mind. How long had the device been watching me?

The drone was about 20 metres above the ground and was taunting me. It probably had a range of several kilometres. Its pilot could be located anywhere, perhaps even outside the exclusion zone.

The aircraft had stabilised a few metres from me, decreasing its altitude. It seemed to be watching me. No doubt about it, I was now sure: the drone had followed me into the Red Forest. I now recognised this metallic sound that had seemed so occult to me. The aircraft emitted a discreet but finely perceptible sound. Its light-gray colour made it invisible, it blended perfectly into this snowy environment. Being rather compact, the device could operate stealthily and sneak through trees. It knew how to avoid obstacles and mastered low-flying. The pilot was obviously experienced. He would have had to accumulate dozens of hours of practice and had the necessary experience to operate in a forest environment. The cameras were staring at me while its small rotors were running at full speed. I grabbed a pine cone and tried to aim at the camera. With a very skilful lateral movement, the drone avoided my shot and then calmly returned to its initial position, ready to resume its observation.

I picked up a stone, a branch, snow, everything I could get my hands on to throw it at the machine. Nothing worked. The drone was dodging peacefully and waiting for my next attempt.

The aircraft was sensitive to movement. I tried to run and then hide behind a tree trunk. The device circled concentrically in the sky, gradually lowering its altitude. It seemed furious that it had lost track of me and was trying in every way to find me. I felt that its pilot was angry. Relieved, I tried not to move, keeping my position, like a soldier ambushed behind enemy lines. I closed my eyes to calm myself. My comfort was short-lived. The slight buzzing of the aircraft was approaching me again. The drone could be sophisticated enough to detect thermal variations and therefore the heat emitted by my body in this icy environment. To avoid this risk, I decided to roll in the snow, covering my skin with powder to my ears in order to build a makeshift camouflage. These efforts were useless. The drone found me in a few minutes and stood over me again. It seemed to be measuring me, its little rotors were twirling around in an evil choreography. I run away from it all the more, throwing all my strength into this new escape. I was slaloming through the woods. My only chance to free myself from its pursuit was to take refuge in the deep forest, where the trees were too close together and the foliage dense enough.

The aircraft could not keep track of me unless it flew at a very low altitude, which made flying extremely difficult because of the increasingly thick bushes and possible snowfall that could damage the drone.

I was at the top of a small hill that gave me a pretty good view of the surroundings. With a breath of fresh air, I descended a little further down the slope. A half-frozen stream flowed down below. The river was crossed by a slight current that prevented it from freezing completely. I jumped off the small stone bridge over it and found myself in the cold, viscous water. I was now less exposed.

The stream was somewhat masked by menacing ferns that I considered my allies. I ignored the branches that whipped my face and kept moving forward. My legs were submerged and I had to fight against the mud and all kinds of plants that slowed my progress. The temperatures were polar, but the adrenaline made me immune to the bitter cold. I finally stopped a few metres further on, where the river was narrowing.

Squatting down as much as possible, I waited for a few long minutes while holding my breath. I listened carefully to distinguish the discreet noise from my pursuer. Nothing.

The silence was insolent. Only the creek's trickling was perceptible. I had won. The drone had lost track of me and probably turned back.

I stayed there for a few minutes shivering. I wasn't even thinking about measuring the radiation level anymore. Perhaps these waters were dangerous? Perhaps these furs were full of rare diseases and bacteria little understood by science? I didn't care about that. I had reached that point where my fears had been prioritised in such a way that the Zone and its dangers were not more than a trivial concern, a distraction at most. The real danger was the people living in this territory, those who were chasing me, but whose nature I didn't know.

I remembered that corpse, that woman they had tried to obliterate. Maybe she had children. Instinctively, I thought of my own mother. Was she missing me?

I realised I had never discussed the disaster with her before. Our common life had been punctuated by unspoken words and a false painless detachment. After my father's death, the subject was no longer discussed. She would never know that I had been to Pripyat. She had always wanted to forget that life. Would I see her again? She didn't seem to want to. After all, it wasn't important. She had almost deserted my memory. I had removed her from my existence. Recent events had followed one another and now represented a disorganised whole. My memories were imperfect, they dispersed and intertwined in a devious dance. I struggled to achieve coherence. I was missing something, an imminent fear was poisoning me.

My phone rang suddenly. Andrei had sent me a message:

'I have terrible news: Amanda is dead! Get out of the Zone, escape from here!'

I was glued to my screen. I reread the short text over and over again. I wanted to keep it in my memory for a long time, and certainly not to forget it. The headaches were coming back, I closed my eyes.

Chapter 8 — Ephemeral

11th day in the Zone.

The place looked familiar to me. It was obvious, I had been here as a child. It was a theatre. I could have sworn it. My memory amazed me. I could easily visualise the appearance of the room and the shape of the seats; however, I had no idea what I had done the day before. Where had I slept? Who had I met? I was unable to remember my last meal. My memories seemed to drown in a misty ocean. My brain refused to make this effort. It was not laziness, but rather a kind of natural veto as if I was biologically programmed not to remember certain events. It didn't matter. The present moment was equally precious. The pungent smell of abandonment that filled my nostrils. The stale, dusty air rushing into my lungs. The precarious ground, whose wobbly parquet surface threatened to tear and drop me to the floor below. These very real sensations occupied my mind and guided me in my quest for exploration. I wanted to deepen my research, to reach beyond.

I left the building. An illegible sign pointed northeast, where many clouds were fighting over the sky. It was appealing. I had to cross a river to get there. The bridge had never been renovated and most of it had collapsed. So I would have to cross the ice.

The frost was significant, I had no doubt about the solidity of the passage. I made a commitment without hesitation. Nevertheless, the accumulated fatigue deprived me of my usual precautions. I had a heavy and clumsy step. My mind was numb, apathetic. The slight cracks on the surface should have caught my attention. The abnormal sounds of the ice cracking should have frightened me. I didn't pay attention to these omens and set out to move forward. My eyes were fixed on the other side, my only objective.

When I was two thirds of the way across, I took a short break, just to catch my breath. I wanted to relax my muscles. I needed a handful of seconds at most. The resumption of my effort was imminent. Suddenly, the ice gave way. Without a warning, I was plunged into water at -3 °C. The river was moderately deep, but the temperature was paralysing me. I was unable to swim and was slowly sinking. My numb limbs were immobile while the ice water burned my face. In a flash of lucidity, I loosened my arms from the straps of my backpack. I also managed to get rid of my jacket that restricted my movements. So I had no choice but to let my things flow into the dark depths. Released, I tried to wiggle my body, to move my legs and arms in order to get back up. I resurfaced with shortness of breath and imploring lungs.

My underwater thrashing had caused the ice blocks around me to break off. It was easier for me to swim to shore now. In a final effort, I reached the shore, clinging to branches to pull myself out of the water.

I was shaking from the cold, hungry and lost. My Geiger counter was condemned, I no longer had any landmarks and could no longer ensure my safety. I now had to progress blindly, without any information about the amounts of radiation to which I was exposed. My shivers of cold slowly turned into ones of terror. The situation was slipping through my fingers once again. By squinting my eyes, I managed to see something in the sky. A chimney spat out a black cloud: human life was there. Exhausted, I fell to my knees in the snow. The blizzard kept me from screaming, from asking for help. My senses were getting weaker. I finally lost consciousness. I felt myself floating in a nebulous dream, where the flakes fell as I slashed at my skin and clothes. The trees swung, crossing over one another, they seemed to be plotting against me. Enigmatic sounds came to me, but I was unable to interpret them.

Was I crazy? Was I dead? Was the Great Journey beginning? How could I begin to think?

I felt my face being sprayed with boiling water. I finally regained consciousness. When I opened my eyes, I was inside a small wooden house, with only two rooms and almost no furniture. A Babushka was facing me, hands on her hips, a scarf on her head. She looked both reassured and mocking. Without any warning, she literally slapped me to bring me to, and brought me a dirty glass filled with a dubious liquid: 'Drink this, poor man!'

Being thirsty and confused, I did so without protest. The unidentified liquid spread down my throat and then into my oesophagus, burning everything in its path. 'Take another one, it can't hurt you!'

I complied again. The drink was unknown, but effective. The alcohol was spreading through my body, creating both a comforting and intense feeling of warmth.

I noticed that my bag was carefully placed against the wall. I thought I had lost it in the water... Was I lucid?

The Babushka was watching me, her forehead wrinkled. Her features were extremely drawn and her face looked rough, but she smiled. She seemed delighted to have a guest. As soon as she saw me blinking my eyelids, she started making herbal teas and slices of bacon. My imperfect Ukrainian and her very heavy accent made communication difficult. However, I hung on, eager to know more. The Babushka was called Yaroslava. She told me about her existence, detailing the daily life in the Soviet Union, the Chernobyl accident, her late husband, the sub-sistence there and the vegetable garden. The events of 1986 were still intact in her weakened memory. She told me about the forced evacuation and her stubborn refusal to obey it. Like her, about 1200 people had chosen to re-turn, sneaking through the barbed wire in defiance of gov-ernment bans. The alternative housing granted was not worth losing their wooden houses, their plots of land, their homes for.

'A lot of people thought we were crazy. The people of Kiev couldn't understand why we wanted to stay. Some considered us only as inhabitants of Chernobyl, rather than full-fledged Ukrainians. My grandchildren are almost forced to hide their origins or they are overwhelmed with ques-tions and comments of all kinds. But I wouldn't trade being

in this place for anything in the world . This is my home,'
she said proudly.

The Babushkas were in their forties at the time of the
disaster. They had chosen to defy rationality by returning to
live in the most toxic place on earth; a space where soil, air
and water would be contaminated for tens of thousands of
years. A space that had seen them born, grow and age.
This territory that they cherished so much would be their
last resting place. Radiation frightened them less than star-
vation, with the Holodomor and the Second World War still
haunting their collective memory.

The Babushkas ensured their survival by growing
vegetables and picking mushrooms. Some even hunted.
Others, like my benefactor, handled the axe perfectly, despite her 83 years of age. The power of the household,
their refusal to abandon their homes and their attachment
to their native lands kept them alive.

She showed me a clipping from a 1997 press article.
Yaroslava and her husband proudly appeared in the photo
accompanying the text, smiling with a wheelbarrow in their
arms. 'In the 1990s, many photographers and journalists
came to visit us. My husband was still alive at that time, he
could help me with the garden,' she explained.

The Babushkas came from these villages and knew
the Zone better than anyone else. They had been there
since their birth. Most of them lived in Kupovatoe, a small
hamlet in the Zone. Today, there were only a handful, ben-
efiting from humanitarian aid, and sometimes receiving visits from soldiers or even tourists. Faced with their visceral

obstinacy, the Ukrainian government had abandoned the idea of dislodging them and was now content to provide them with occasional medical assistance so that they could end their lives with dignity.

'The Zone had regained a very ordinary pace of life. We sowed the fields and ploughed with the same vigour as before. Some of us felt invigorated by overcoming the evacuations. After all, we had taken our destiny into our own hands. We had stayed. We were stronger than the others. We were not afraid of the setbacks of science. Radioactivity or none, we would never abandon our land. Autumns passed, winters extended and we savoured our decision. We were aware that we were individuals apart, forgotten. Politicians don't care about us, they had a lot of other worries anyway.'

She did not seem to have ignored the revolutionary events of 2014. She told me about her family, her cousin who left for the Soviet Navy at the age of 18. He had been stationed in Sevastopol in the Crimea, but had died long before the annexation. His children now lived not far from Odessa.

'They have a very different daily life from ours. Here, we fight every day for our survival. But I'm not complaining. I chose to come back, it's where I belong. Sometimes I think about what my life would have been like if I had run away. Life in Ukraine today is really difficult, but it was much worse 50 years ago.'

The Holodomor and the war had decimated the population. The trauma was still present and inspired many popular songs. Her grandchildren did not know the Soviet Union. This troubled period had dissolved before they were born. The fall of the USSR had raised hopes for a profound change in Ukrainian society and an improvement in living conditions. She explained to me that little had really changed, at least not to the extent of the expectations that had been raised: 'People are still poor, corruption is omnipresent and great Russia is watching fiercely!'

When asked if she had already left the Zone, Yaroslava laughed and coughed: 'What for? There's nothing for me outside. And then, who would feed the dogs, who would take care of the vegetable garden? No and no, I'm staying here. It's where I belong.'

The comfort of the house was rudimentary, but it was rather well maintained. A picture of her daughter's wedding was hanging over the fireplace.

The hearth was bright red, almost hypnotic. The Babushka mastered the secrets of fire better than I did. I was impressed by her autonomy and resourcefulness. She told me that every morning she was busy extracting water from the well. A practice, of course, not recommended by the authorities, but she did not mind. Every day, Yaroslava was making the same tireless movements, pressing the valve to fill her small scrap bucket. Her children had bought her an electric kettle, which was plugged into the only outlet in the house. Various multicoloured embroideries and orthodox icons adorned the different shelves.

Yaroslava explained to me that once a year, she and the others were entitled to a visit to the church of Ivankiv, located about forty kilometres from her village. Buses were specially chartered. It was every year, a real expedition, a moment they all looked forward to, as a reward for their survival. They could pray and meet the pope, a rebel too. The church had been renovated and was just as smart as some of the city buildings. All these joyful individuals formed a rather original community and gathered to light candles and celebrate Orthodox festivities. These octogenarians were   small, self-sufficient survivors in the area considered to be one of the most dangerous in the world.

The vast majority of Babushkas lived alone, their husbands having died. Their social relationships were therefore restricted to the few individuals who ventured there and to other Babushkas living nearby. Some of them had a family living outside the Zone. Sometimes they were fortunate enough to have their grandchildren visit them. Not everyone was so lucky. But they did not complain, stating that they were even happier than those who had accepted the evacuation.

'Babushka is no longer young. The survivors are dropping like flies. One after the other, they all go. The men went long ago. I wish to take my last breath here, not in a concrete hospital outside. My children are almost gone. I just hope they will take care of burying me in my garden... Government visits are also becoming more and more rare. They're barely giving us any more money. Not so long ago, scientists came here. They took eggs and water from the well. They shipped their samples to a laboratory in Kiev. If it can help them...'

'Do you often receive guests like me?'

'No, unfortunately. Sometimes tourists come here, but it's very rare. Usually, they just want a picture. Some of the guides I know come by to say hello to me from time to time. I make them pancakes and we chat.'

'What do you think about this treasure thing?'

She laughed as she moved.

'Nonsense, kiddo, nonsense. There is no treasure. None of this ever existed. You want some more soup? I also have beans for you.'

'Thank you for being so kind, but I have to go now.'

'Don't forget your bag!'

I packed my things and left the house. In the garden, a pig was in a small enclosure. He waited knowingly to be slaughtered and looked at me with his dull little eyes.

The Babushka handed me supplies, insisting for the umpteenth time that I stay a few more days. She'd cook me pancakes and recite Slavic songs. I politely refused while thanking her warmly for her help. I was refreshed and alive. It was time to go on a journey.

I slowly walked away, a little disturbed by this unexpected encounter and my mind fogged up by the alcohol she had been administering to me all the time. With her axe in hand, Yaroslava shouted at me and let me turn my heels.

I continued on my way without a precise destination. The Babushka's statements about the treasure had disturbed, but I was not discouraged. A mad hope was still burning in me. Despite the events, I paradoxically felt more serene than at the beginning of my expedition. My belongings were finally safe and secure, the bag wasn't even wet and the Geiger counter seemed to work. I didn't know what could have caused this miracle. Could the Babushka have extracted it from the water?

There were now many paths open to me. I picked one at random and tried to follow it as far as I was able.

Chapter 9 — Bitterness

13th day in the Zone.

I had been walking for several hours and I slowly became exhausted, forcing me to slow down. The night-mares of the night had diminished me. Moreover, this part of the forest was totally unknown to me. No particular mention had been made of it on the maps I had previously examined. My observations of the sun indicated to me that I had headed north. I explored blindly. I was captivated by the unexpected nature of my discoveries.

The woodland ornaments followed one another in a splendid fresco of which I was the witness. The atmosphere was strange, the forest seemed lethargic, almost asleep. The calm was deafening, even my boots didn't make the snow crunch.

A fierce cry resounded. My pulse accelerated suddenly. I barely had time to turn around when I was thrown to the ground in a burst of fury. It was him.

He roared again.

The blows were raining down. I lay at his feet like a wounded animal that would be shot and then displayed like a trophy. Dazed, I got up as best I could. I was surprised he let me do this. Maybe he was willing to talk? Were negotiations possible? No, he had other plans for me. He grabbed me violently against a tree trunk, cracking the bark while scratching my flesh. The entire ground vibrated under the impact. His dark eyes were staring at me, threatening and motionless. He didn't say any words, just fixed me in his stare. An infinite sadness was emerging from his face. I assumed that a firm and strong hand would smash my nose any second, but he just let go. I fell backwards, at his feet again. Still on his feet, he suddenly turned on his heels and walked away, his silhouette disappearing through the icy mist.

I waited a few minutes for my weakness to dissipate before going after him, following his tracks preserved by the snow.

I thought I had lost him for good when I saw a kind of hut, blended in with its surroundings. I had found the Howler, and better still, I had reached his hut.

It was a legend, a myth that the Stalkers liked to tell when they shared cigarettes. Amanda had told me about it, I was almost certain. Few people had actually observed him and even fewer had met him. According to reports, a journalist from Kiev had approached him one day and convinced him to conduct an interview. A story like that would have made the headlines in the tabloid press and would have been relayed around the world via the Internet. But that never happened. The interview might have been completed, but it was never published, as the author categorically refused to do so, without providing any explanation.

Like the Babushkas, the Howler lived on agriculture, fruit picking, hunting and fishing. However, unlike them, he had chosen isolation in a true sense. Human relationships no longer interested him. They made no sense to him.

While the Babushkas rejoiced in every social contact and welcomed the walkers with hospitality, he was terribly misanthropic. His autarchy was almost total. His life on the margins of rationality was a mystery that I wanted to decipher.

In an unresentful manner, I chose to visit him, determined to get to know my aggressor. He opened the door for me before I even had to indicate my presence. Our first meeting seemed forgotten, as his initial violence contrasted with his sudden cordiality. He had arranged his shack in a fairly comfortable way. He had lots of books. Stacked in a random and disorderly manner, they were a kind of homely wall decoration. The place was comforting despite its primitive characteristics. It was even supplied with electricity.

'It only works for a few hours a day, but it's more than enough,' he said with a faint smile. 'Coffee, tea?'

The Howler was stocky and endowed with a penetrating gaze. His shaggy and neglected appearance made him look like an old man. He no longer took care of his looks. It was pointless, no one was supposed to meet him, he had no one to impress. One fact troubled me: he was almost the same age as my father. His daughter had been born in Pripyat, in the large hospital where my mother worked. The small family then moved to Kharkiv. The Howler told me his misfortunes: his only child had died of rubella, and his wife had killed herself the next day. According to her suicide note, she had attached herself to a bag full of stones and then jumped into the river. Her body had never been recovered.

After the death of his daughter and wife, the Howler had fallen into severe depression. His heart had become as hard as a stone. Every material possession, every dream of prosperity became futile and insipid. Images of his past, of his then happy existence, haunted him. Nostalgia had poisoned him and was slowly attacking him. The abundance of happiness that was exuded by everyone around him made him anxious. He wanted to escape the peace of others. He had therefore chosen to return to find the only thing he had left, his native land.

'My anchor in this world,' he said.

Only loneliness helped him to survive. If he hadn't come home, he'd already be dead.

'My daily life was all about hesitating between hanging myself and gunshot suicide. I was exhausted,' he explained.

As our discussion progressed, I felt that I was gaining his trust. He didn't hate me in particular and I understood that he needed to talk. I made him my friend, there are too few of them in the Zone. So I decided to spend several days with him. I wanted to learn, exchange ideas, and above all understand his way of life.

The Howler's daily life was structured by simple but essential activities. He would pick blueberries from the undergrowth, weave his way through swamps or climb trees to catch the horizon and decipher the stars. His bestial appearance contrasted with his naturally calm and curious personality. He knew everything about the world he lived in, listening to the radio and reading books brought back to him by the military. He knew perfectly well the company he had sought to desert. He frequently travelled through Pripyat, but only at night so as to remain discreet and make the place his own. It was the only remedy against the voracious melancholy that consumed him. His nostalgia was still vivacious, it was the only emotion that kept him alive. This inexhaustible need to contemplate his past, to relive through memory the glorious hours of his family, his childhood, these happy times.

The Howler had a boat, a kind of raft with an old engine and oars that allowed him to go up the Pripyat River. From time to time, he decided to travel through the Zone. He roamed the river alone, having no course but the desire to drift. The engine was broken, but the paddles were fine.

'The soldiers leave you alone?' I asked.

'Oh yes, our interactions are even quite friendly when we meet. But they hardly pass through anymore. They have enough to worry about with the protection of the Zone and the surveillance of the Stalkers. And then there's this damn war in the east.'

'And the tourists? Any of them make it this far?'

'One of them came to my hut once. He wanted to take pictures of me from different angles. I threw his camera in the river. He didn't dare get it back.'

'Are you planning to stay around until the end?'

'The Babushkas are all old. In 5 or 6 years, I will be the last here and I intend to be the last native of Pripyat to die in the Zone. That's where I belong, next to my daughter.'

'And the danger?' I asked him.

'What danger? What danger? Cold, hunger, loneliness. That is the real danger. The Babushkas in the cities live in concrete hutches. Here, they are free, queens in their own lands. You know that the post-traumatic stress of evacuations had consequences as serious as the disaster itself. No, no and no. I'm much better off here.'

As the hours passed, I felt that the Howler appreciated me, in contrast to the circumstances of our meeting. I decided to launch the subject of the treasure:

'Is it true what they say? A treasure is buried somewhere in the Zone?'

He thought for a moment and sighed.

'You know, I've seen others. Not so long ago, a man came all the way here to meet me about it. He was rather imposing and looked dark. He seemed tormented as if a curse was hanging over him. If you ask me, your obsession will defeat you all.'

'That's not why I came here. The subject just arouses my curiosity, that's all.'

'Nonsense, they all say that. They actually have only one concern: to find the damn treasure. I'd shoot them one by one if I could.'

He grumbled:

'Why don't they just enjoy their miserable lives instead of trying to find something here! There is nothing for them. Death awaits them and will take them like all the others. You know, I got the fortune. Prosperity, family, all these components of happiness were mine.'

The desolation that shrouded his face seemed irremediable to me. The hope once present in his eyes seemed to have evaporated forever. He was condemned to live with this loneliness, which he himself had chosen. No one had imposed this painful exile on him. I still had the impression that living as a hermit softened his suffering. He told me how looters had ransacked his daughter's grave. Without shame, they had exhumed the body in search of clues that could lead to Pripyat's treasure. Furious at having failed, after desecrating the tomb they had abandoned it in the forest, like a common rubbish.

'I only caught one. The kid begged and begged for forgiveness. I didn't think about it. I took my axe and split his skull from top to bottom. I dumped what was left of his body in the river. Most of his friends had already fled. Others attended the scene. They swore they'd kill me sooner or later. I am waiting for them almost as much as death.'

The Howler frowned as he prepared his hook. He performed this operation with great precision and without distraction. The movements were mastered and the choreography turned out perfect. He took a few steps forward and dipped his fishing rod into the water before sitting on the ground.

'Some fish are huge, you'll see.'

'Are they really bigger since the accident?'

'It's hard to say. Probably. Anyway, they're much better. The river is less polluted than in the past. I suppose they are in excellent health. In the past, people used to dump a whole lot of waste. No one cared about water quality.'

'Are you angry?'

'Against whom?'

I pointed towards the power plant.

'The people who built this.'

'No. No. We needed it. I have no particular resentment against the government of the day. I hate both the whole world and myself.'

The Howler pulled in his fishing rod and then threw it to the ground with an angry look. Apparently, the fish didn't want to bite. He gave up.

'Never mind, I'm going swimming. Are you coming?'

I nodded. The water must have been just over 0 °C, not to mention its radioactive nature. The Howler undressed and dived in totally naked. He glided away nonchalantly, disappearing into the nascent mist. As for me, I decided to go back to his shack. Entering it without its owner gave me the sensation of rediscovering it. The place was usually impregnable. It was strongly defended by the Howler who hardly let anyone in. I was favoured, I had won his trust. Did I deserve it?

I pushed the door, my heart pounding, and stepped into the hut. It was warm, silent and disorderly. I looked through his library. The Howler had all kinds of books: biology textbooks, political essays and even epistemology books; he did not spare himself any discipline. A manuscript bound with cords caught my attention. It was a collection of letters with no date or signature on them. The calligraphy seemed shaky and I had trouble deciphering it. In addition, the paper was damaged, some lines were missing and made the story particularly frustrating:

'The situation is very tense. The magma has pierced the concrete slab that separates the core from the reactor that melts with the water. According to Nesterenko, there is a risk of a 4-megaton nuclear explosion. (*Unreadable...*) Workers were hastily requisitioned. I had no choice. But I do what I'm told. (*Unreadable...*) The guys are all pretty young. Most of them are barely older than kids. The oldest of them is 32 years old. There are nearly 10,000 of them working in shifts all the time. Some are from Donbass, others from Tula in Russia. They were promised a reward. A lot of them would have gone there without it. They probably don't know what they're risking. I myself don't have much information about it. Some workers work without protection. Not all of them have adequate masks or clothing. I even saw some in shorts with bare chests. The heat is extreme down there. We were not able to install any ventilation ducts through the underground. Temperatures reach 50 degrees. (*Unreadable...*) I just carry out the orders.'

On another page:

'Now the gallery is 150 metres long and has been completed. The mission is accomplished. The guys are relieved. But we remain cautious, the worst is still to be avoided. (*Unreadable...*) The situation in Moscow is critical. I've heard some pretty serious things. Hospital number 6 is overcrowded. I've had horrible scenes described to me.

Western journalists are being kept out of the picture. No one must know. (*Unreadable...*) But miners are not the only heroes. Successive helicopter pilots are facing an extremely difficult situation. We have 80 aircrafts that take turns to contain the radioactive fumes coming from the reactor. They were brought from Siberia, 4,000 km away from Chernobyl. The guys are doing a fabulous job, but not everything is going as we would like. Yesterday because of the heat and radiation one of the pilots fainted in the middle of the flight. Fortunately, the helicopter was rescued by the first officer. Others were less fortunate. We're trying to keep it a secret, but an MI -8 crashed during operations. Of course there are no survivors. I look forward to returning to Kopyliv.'

Many pages awaited me, but I heard the Howler returning. His heavy step and hoarse voice seemed very close. With my heart pounding, I closed the manuscript. It probably contained other exciting stories. I decided to steal the document by hiding it under my jacket.

'Guess who I saw...'

'Who?' I replied in a candid voice.

'Oleksandr. I saw him in the distance.'

'What's he doing around here?'

'I have no idea. If he had come near me, I swear on my head I would have strangled him.'

'Why do you hate each other so much?'

'Old quarrels... But you must know that Oleksandr is a little disturbed. And then ... he's a coward. He fears himself. He can be very impulsive. In fact, he has already fought in the Zone with Egor, another vagrant. It is said that it was so violent that they had to be beaten to calm them down. They really had a hard time separating them.'

'Who are they?'

'Other troubled spirits you don't know.'

He moaned into his beard.

'All crazy, they're all crazy. I don't understand why you're staying here.'

'You yourself have remained,' I objected.

He grumbled, saying a few incomprehensible words. I watched him walking away to his room in his characteristic gait, the stagger of a learned and bruised old man.

I left the hut to settle on the steps. The vantage point offered a sparkling horizon. Winter was coming to an end. The Chernobyl plains would soon be covered with flowers and dazzling lights. Green and golden hues would follow the implacable whiteness of the cold nights that raged here. Przewalski's horses would gallop through the vast depopulated areas, where they would encounter lynx, foxes and wolves also enjoying a habitat deserted by man. Europe's original ecosystem would thrive and I would no longer be there to contemplate it. Why should I leave?

Chapter 10 — *Jupiter*

21st day in the Zone.

I arrived at the Jupiter factory, a vast tangle of steel structures, dilapidated buildings and abandoned trucks. The place had an aura of secrecy. Officially, the main objective of the factory was to make video recorders and radio components. However, its unofficial use was to provide the Soviet army with strategic equipment. Components necessary for submarines or the space industry were assembled here. You could still see a satellite dish on the roof of the complex. Some even thought that the plant was producing electronic components embedded in the USSR's nuclear missiles.

The factory was the second-largest employer in the exclusion zone after the nuclear power plant. It had continued to operate after the disaster and was only abandoned years later. The site had been converted into a radiation monitoring and decontamination process management centre. In particular, it tested the robots used to manufacture the temporary enclosure around the reactor. It was one of the largest buildings in the Zone. However, it was not on the guided tour program, due to its poor condition and the risk of roof collapse. Thus, the general public was relatively unaware of its existence. On the other hand, the Stalkers were very familiar with the Jupiter factory. For my part, it was the first time I had been there. I felt a little thrill of excitement, the same one that had accompanied me when I entered the Azure pool.

The complex was not difficult to reach, the plant was located southeast of Yanov and was easily accessible without means of transport. All you had to do was follow Zavodska Street on the outskirts of Pripyat. I was convinced that I knew the path even though I had never taken it. For a strange reason, the surroundings seemed familiar to me. There were some rusty, rundown minibuses in front of the entrance to the complex. Some rested on their sides as if an invisible force had tipped them over to prevent their use.

The plant was only abandoned in 1996. It was still full of industrial equipment and scientific apparatus. Inside, the machines had been dismantled and the spare parts sold elsewhere. Many areas had been converted into living spaces. Thus, one could find sofas, books and flowerpots scattered all over the place in an almost charming disorder.

The main building had a cellar that aroused strong curiosity among the stalkers. Nevertheless, I did not venture to explore the basement of the plant because of its recent flooding. Who knew what kind of horrors could thrive there? So I limited myself to walking around the ground floor and the upper floors.

I looked through the main room: the ground was strewn with debris, mostly just rubbish. An imposing ventilation duct was attached to the wall. Its silver colour gave it a stylish appearance despite the ravages of time. I tried to discover whether a man could sneak in. Probably a small person would be able to. In an adjacent corridor, I found a sign detailing the rotation schedules for workers. I continued my progress up the stairs, wandering according to my intuitions.

Andrei had mentioned this place only a few times. The only thing he'd told me was that he had been shot in the area. Strangely enough, it didn't scare me. I had confidence in the place, I didn't feel threatened. I was even wondering if Andrei had lied. It was his style to dramatise and distort reality to make himself seem more exhilarating. As for me, I was not carrying any weapons and had no need to protect myself from anything.

A little further on, I walked through a thick door to find myself in a rectangular room, the floor of which was entirely covered with mosses. Marks on the wall suggested that a radiator had been ripped off. In an underlying room, a large ruby-red safe lay discarded in a corner. It was half-opened, but, of course, empty of any content. I tried to imagine what kinds of secrets might have been stored there, scientific and industrial mysteries that had probably been destroyed or even stolen.

My eyes were drawn to a can of soda that was lying in the middle of the filth. It looked brand new. Its light-blue colour was bright and barely covered with dust. I turned my head carefully to find more evidence of recent visits. Some abandoned shoes were piled up, but it was impossible for me to date them. I was about to approach them when I noticed a rather characteristic sound. It was not a scream or laughter, but rather a lament. Someone was

sobbing. The pace was slow and deep. The tone was unusual. It was male crying. The swallowing was accompanied by quite serious sighs, with tragic tendencies. Slowly, I
tried to follow it. I could not distinguish the individual, only
my hearing guided my steps.

I walked through a door and saw him. The man was
lying on the ground, slumped against a wall, his hands
joined on his head as a sign of torture. I couldn't believe it,
but it was Oleksandr. That unfeeling and unfathomable
colossus was now in a position of incredible weakness.
Contrasting thoughts were going through me. Should I
comfort him, run away, kill him? My intuition was screaming at me to get out of there, but I was still petrified. I was
trying to understand what could have put him in this state.

While these thoughts went through my head, I was
struck by the fact that Oleksandr was standing between
me and the exit. There was no way I could let him see me.
His reaction would be too unpredictable. I thought fast before I realised the obvious. The windows were my only escape. I was on the second floor. A jump was possible, the
deep snow would cushion the fall. Oleksandr had for-
midable senses, I was convinced he would hear me. I took
one last look at him. He was starting to stir. He blew his
nose noisily and then staggered up. He was heading towards me. I swore silently. No more choices: I approached
the opening of the adjoining window and jumped through
it. The time spent in the air seemed endless to me. The
landing was violent. I had jumped in a hurry, without worrying about what was underneath. In addition, I had chosen

the worst window, given the presence of a small fir tree nearby. Though it helped to slow my fall, it also slapped my face. Branches had skewered my shoulders, thorns had whipped my face, but I had managed not to make any sound. My heart was racing, but I was intact.

I was worried for a few seconds about whether Oleksandr had heard me. How would he have reacted if he had seen me?

I walked away hurriedly, limping slightly. My own dazzling energy surprised me. I almost felt like the roles had been reversed between me and Oleksandr. I was troubled by his change of character. I didn't think he had the capacity for suffering, he who was so austere and detached. As for me, I felt more and more comfortable to evolve in the Zone; at least I was trying to convince myself of that. The days I spent here had hardened me. My survival instinct, my resistance to the physical elements, all this had developed recently. On the other hand, I was well aware that my memory problems had become worse. I preferred to ignore this deficiency because it affected me so much. I forced myself to deny this deep weakness. Dwelling on it plunged me into a dark sadness, which enveloped virulent remorse. I chose to ignore it, to live with these mental omissions.   It was in this raging state of mind that I walked for hours. I wanted to find my one and only ally here, the Howler.

I quickly reached his hut. He welcomed me as a faithful friend, handing me food and blankets while listening to my story without interruption. In the end, he just sighed and shrugged.

'You tire me. You'd better leave, I don't know what's keeping you here. These bastards will destroy your mind. Maybe it's already too late. You grew up here, but you don't have to die here. Leave them in their madness. Give them up to their obsessions. Go back to your previous life.'

'But still... I don't understand. They seem to need me. And then Oleksandr is a riddle. The other two as well. I have trouble understanding them.'

'You know, I knew Oleksandr well. There was a time when we were almost friends. He used to walk around the Zone, accompanied by some visitors. Sometimes he would bring me supplies or equipment for my shack and then at night we would play cards together. He never seemed to want to go home, constantly postponing the time to leave... It is true that he was not very talkative. As the seasons passed, his visits became rarer. We gradually lost contact. To be honest, I don't care what happened to him. It doesn't look good anyway. As for the other two, I can't tell you anything. I don't really know them. They seem smart, but I'm not sure what the hell they're doing here. They are running to their doom. Like you, by the way.'

He sighed as he stroked his beard. He looked like someone who had talked too much and was now satisfied with the silence. After a few minutes, he finally took the floor again:

'I'm sick of your stories, you're driving me crazy. You can stay here for the night, but tomorrow go away for good. I hope you never see me again. I've already buried enough people.'

As soon as his last words were spoken, he disappeared behind a thick red curtain. A few minutes later, I heard him snore to the rhythm of the wind. As for me, I was thinking. I felt trapped in a decision that was beyond me. I was thinking about Oleksandr. How could I fear this man who had saved my life? If he hadn't taken me out of the Red Forest, I would have stayed there dead from cold or exhaustion. If I was really his enemy, he had had the opportunity to let me disappear. On the other hand, he seemed to be watching over me while the other two were dragging me into their crazy plans. I was starting to hate them. The more time I spent with them, the more they seemed unreliable and untrustworthy. They had convinced me to embark on their adventure, their damn treasure hunt. I hadn't asked for anything. That's not why I came here. I had to talk to them, stop all this. I didn't even know why I'd agreed to join them in the first place anymore. I cleared my throat by letting another swear word burst out. I felt hateful towards all of them. It was decided, I would stop this fuss. Tomorrow I'd talk to Amanda about it and escape from here.

***

The day after tomorrow.

When I reached the top of the tree, I scanned the horizon. The landscape stretched out in front of me in absolute calm. The silence was total. Not a single sound dis-

162

turbed the environment. No bird cries, no insect rustling. Not a single breath of wind. Just nothingness.

I tried to see through the darkness. The river widened as it moved northward. Small, ice-covered streams meandered around, connecting to one another. A multitude of pine trees stood before my eyes. They were beautiful, and seemingly infinite to me.

The Howler's hut was camouflaged, but visible to anyone who knew of its existence. It was high enough to prevent easy access, but too little hidden to prevent observation. You had to climb about ten metres on a suspended ladder of dubious solidity in order to reach the hut. I thought that its occupant was probably sleeping at this late hour. With the help of a few stars, I managed to see his boat lying below. It was laid on the ground, nonchalantly and in plain sight.

I went down from my observation point to the shore. I pushed the raft with a thousand precautions. I was afraid of disturbing the water, of ruining the perfect quietude. The current was light, the conditions almost ideal. I glided on the river towards the reactor. Its luminous glow guided me. It was my landmark in this marshy maze. Orientation in such an environment was not easy. I had to be on my guard. One mistake and I would find myself at a checkpoint, where a handful of sluggish soldiers would be happy to stop me and blackmail me to give back my freedom.

Lying on my boat, I was slow but powerful in my rowing movements. I approached the nuclear complex. No sound came to me. The reactor was totally silent. It was a disconcerting sight given its dimensions and imposing lighting. My mind seemed to want to hear sounds, sounds of men getting busy, roars of machines being operated. In fact, I could almost perceive the steam that should have come out of the cooling column.

Was my mind playing tricks on me? Yes, of course, but I liked it. This almost tangible vision soothed me. It delighted me to think that Chernobyl could have succeeded. After all, it was only a succession of avoidable events that led to the disaster. Like the sinking of the Titanic, the Chernobyl tragedy was part of a long process from the design of the machine to the improper execution of the final operations. Since then, the defective gears had had to be studied and dissected by specialists. All of society had learned from these mistakes and emerged wiser as a result. At least, I had high hopes of it.

My daydreams were swept away in a single moment when I saw the huge structure still under construction. The cooling tower was truly sumptuous. Andrei had not hesitated to call it a piece of art. It was never finished and stood proudly, dominating the river in a flamboyant manner.

I decided to go there. I had never entered such a building before and knew little about how it worked. Was it dangerous? Probably not...

I docked calmly on the shore, tying my raft to an iron post that stuck out of the water. The cooling column was very close and easily accessible. I was very eager to visit this giant with its almost ancient appearance. The entrance was only a few metres away.

Inside the building, every sound resonated, the echo of my footsteps broke the silence with their metallic clattering. The cooling tower was of the hyperboloid type. It culminated in a spherical opening, which gave the impression of observing the sky through a long telescope. The remaining parts were hidden from my view by construction.

The tower was comforting. There was a sense of security, surrounded by the huge concrete column that seemed to rise to the stars. My gaze could be peacefully lost in the infinite stellar universe.

Feeling sleep take over me, I knelt in the grass to finally spread my arms and fall asleep serenely.

I was awakened by the first light of day. I was barely standing when strong headaches began raging inside me. The atmosphere of the place seemed totally different to me. The night had changed my perception of the environment. The humidity was now tenacious and unpleasant. I was going through an experience that was radically different from the previous day. Anguish had taken over from wonder. Methadone boxes were lying on the ground, and the air stank of urine. The structure around me looked like it was threatening to collapse and stimulated my claustrophobia. Why had I slept here?

I hurried out of the tower to walk towards the shore. I had not even considered this eventuality, but it hit me hard: the raft had disappeared. I had firmly secured it, the force of the water alone could not have pulled it away. Someone must have stolen it during the night…

It was still very early, the light was low and the workers' day had not started. I could take the overland route that led directly to the reactor and its sarcophagus. Yes, but the dogs ... those damn gatekeepers would spot me and jump on me. My skin would be lacerated, my face bruised by bites. No, no and no. No way was I considering that option. There was still the river. After all, the distance to the other side was manageable. The current was very low. It was possible.

The headache was threatening again. Like a vulture, it hovered over me, delaying my decision. I took a long breath before throwing my head in first. The shock was severe. I violently pierced the icy water, submerging my body and extending my arms to finally reach the opposite shore, my limbs sore, but safe and sound.

I was thinking about that damn raft... Who took it? I had to take it back to the Howler. He would certainly hate me for it. I didn't want to upset him. He was probably the person I appreciated most in the Zone, the person in whom I had placed the little trust I was able to have.

I thought about admitting to him the evil that was plaguing me. He would not judge my paranoia or increasing schizophrenia. Maybe he could help me? Maybe he would know how to fix my memory. I had my doubts, but I was trying to convince myself. I kept in me this thin hope, this naive will to find a way out, to alleviate my distress. I wanted to eradicate the violence that lay within me. I was undecided. This state of hesitation made me anxious. Finally, I opted for wisdom, I chose to go talk to him. I went to his cabin with my heart gasping and my clothes soaking wet. He was absent.

Chapter 11 — Solution

23rd day in the Zone.

Andrei had not left the Zone. He seemed very nervous when I joined him at the meeting place. He was chewing his gum in a frenetic and exasperating way. His attitude irritated me. He called out to me:

'Did you have a good morning?'

I could tell from the sound of his voice that he didn't care about the answer. His tone was off and his smile seemed forced. He was projecting camaraderie, but I could feel that a certain tension was driving him.

'To be honest, I am thinking of leavingthe Zone. I'll come back later, probably in the fall.'

Obviously, my uncertainty did not seem to appease him. His nervousness seemed to have increased in intensity.

'Look, I'm not sure that's a good idea. We started something; now we have to finish it, and this before the end of winter. After that, hordes of tourists will come and it will probably be too late. Especially since we are not the only ones looking.'

'Yes, of course, but...'

'We trusted you,' Andrei cut in. 'Oleksandr was initially reluctant, but I immediately believed in you. I'm the reason you're with us. You owe me gratitude.'

'Okay, maybe, but … wait a minute, you're working with Oleksandr now? I don't understand, do you…'

'At this point, we can no longer afford to fail!'

'You know, I do have an existence outside. I didn't really come to the Zone for that!'

He whistled loudly and became threatening:

'So that's it, you're going to go back to your little life as a wealthy man, take care of your brilliant career and let us die here? You supposedly came to investigate the Stalkers, but the truth is you yourself became one. We told you our secrets, we trusted you. Now all you're gonna do is write your article and wallow in your miserable little life? No, believe me. You will never stop being haunted by your nightmares. The evil you suffer from will survive. Sooner or later, you'll regret this decision. Your anguish will chase you down. Never, oh no, you will never be at peace! I remind you that Amanda is dead!'

His eyes were dark and his eyebrows furrowed. I remained concrete in the face of his provocations. He continued:

'Who took you for a ride in the Zone? Who took you to the hospital basement? Who saved your life by pulling you out of the Red Forest? No, believe me, you'd be better off staying with us.'

I was at the very least confused. I didn't know how to react and my discomfort was noticeable.

'What exactly do you want from me? I thought you weren't interested in the treasure?'

'You know very well what we're looking for. Help us, that's all we're asking you to do. Trust me, it's the best thing to do if you want to get out of here alive.'

I remained silent. I was a little surprised by the tone of our conversation. Was this the same person who had accompanied me during my debut in the Zone? He offered me a cigarette, almost as a sign of appeasement in order to mitigate my vindictive silence. I felt both angry and guilty. After all, it's true that I owed him a lot. I felt like a stowaway, an illegitimate explorer, who did not deserve to take part in this exciting treasure hunt to which I had been invited.

Basically, I should leave. It was so easy. I had no kind of influence here. Life would go on. Every morning, the dawn would rise over the Red Forest. The big wheel sitting on its steel legs would watch over the city, stoic in the wind, without emitting the slightest sign of weakness, without producing the slightest squeak. Duga would keep its mystery and aura of secrecy. The Azure pool would keep in it the memories of thousands of children, including myself. The proud and elderly Babushkas would perish peacefully near the plots, their homes that they had never consented to abandon. As for me, I would leave. It would be a pitiful debacle, yes, but I would quit the Zone. I'd go back to where I'd run away from. I would face the morbid daily life that I had wanted to forget. And I would win. Yes, I think I would succeed. At least I would survive. I wouldn't kill myself, I didn't have the courage.

Andrei had left and abandoned me to my dilemma. Above me, the sky was threatening. The croaking of crows irritated me. I had always hated those creatures. They were probably happier than me.

I brooded tirelessly. Andrei was a coward. He was a weak spirit governed by a lack of courage. He wanted to succeed without getting involved. He was no better than Oleksandr. Both had only tried to influence me to reach their own ends. I hated them; yes, I despised them. I didn't need them.

I grabbed a branch and smashed it on my knee to break it. 'Fuck them,' I exclaimed as I clenched my teeth. The rage was spreading inside me like a virus. I picked up a second branch and crushed it against a trunk with all the anger I could handle. Sweat was running down my forehead. The headaches were back. Carried away by the anger, I had bitten my lips. My teeth had pierced the flesh so hard that blood dripped to the ground. The once pure snow was now stained by my fury.

My anger took a few minutes to fade. My ears were picking something up. A quiet sound was approaching. I heard footsteps. Boots crunched in the snow. The process was slow, confident. A silhouette was approaching. The individual was dressed in a beige Chapka that almost completely masked his face. Lurking in a bush, I tried to take shallow breaths. The man was on the phone, but I couldn't clearly distinguish his words. He turned his back on me and sat in the snow with his hands together. He seemed to think for a few minutes and then got up, and started to pace. His indecision contrasted with his apparent calm. He finally put his bag on the ground, and took out a small silver drone which he launched with ease. The machine was extremely quiet. It was important not to lose sight of it; otherwise it was difficult to detect. I immediately recognised the aircraft. It was the one which had been watching me when I buried the body, the same as the one in the Red Forest. I tried delicately to get away.

As I retreated, I started thinking, trying to come up with some coherent reasoning. Amanda was also on the treasure trail. She had studied the subject for years and learned a lot. Originally from Cologne, she regularly planned trips to the Zone. The lure of adventure attracted her much more than profit. She knew exactly what she was doing and didn't take any ill-considered risks. She had studied physics at university and had the right equipment to play in the exclusion zone. Oleksandr had grown up in Poland. He was fluent in German and had been able to get in touch with her easily. His skill as a former guide must have given Amanda confidence because he knew the Zone so well. Their collaboration could facilitate their research, their common ambition. Andrei had always seemed elusive to me. Yet he had introduced me to all the facets of his personality. Sometimes jovial, sometimes sinister, he was often friendly, perhaps even sincere. He seemed very confident but also completely lost. I couldn't figure it out. I thought about the nature of his relationship with Amanda. It was troubled, as was the one he had with Oleksandr. I had never really had confirmation of the link between these three…

I had immediately noticed Oleksandr's worried look from the moment we met in that damn bar in Kiev. I was suddenly filled with paranoia. The person who introduced me to the Zone, the one who guided my first steps, may have manipulated me. A shiver ran down my spine. What was my role in it all? What piece of the puzzle was I? I was trying to gather my memories. Nothing obvious came to me. Reminiscences, when you hunt them down, are always able to escape. They were swept away in this ever more violent whirlwind, this inexorable mass of pain with which I was trying to fight. The suffering was both physical and psychological. Concentrated within my very skull, it gave me no chance. Every day I was moving further away from the salvation I sought.

I was thinking about the corpse I buried. Was Oleksandr responsible? Was I really capable of something like that? Could I have forgotten something about it? The sweat was soaking my face. I felt that I held the key to the enigma. Part of me knew the solution. The ultimate obstacle was myself.

It is easy to manipulate others, but cheating your own mind is a different matter. The undertaking is difficult and highly schizophrenic. We must measure our weaknesses, tame our darkness and dominate our reason. My subconscious housed the answer. I had to force it by any means necessary.

Who else held the secret of my situation? Was my amnesiac condition perceptible? I was convinced that Andrei knew. Amanda must have told him. She had detected it so quickly...

I walked along the path like a condemned man, my arms dangling, and my head down. Ruminations turned into deep despair. I hated myself for forgetting, I despised myself for existing. My suicidal thoughts were interrupted by the vibrations of my phone. Someone wanted to call me. The number was hidden. I answered. A calm and hoarse voice uttered these three words:

'*Jäta või sureke*'.

The conversation was immediately cut off. I could not identify the language used, but the tone was threatening and unequivocal. Each syllable seemed to be shooting at me. Once again, the spectre of fear was spreading. Around me, the snowfall was intensifying. I turned off my phone for good and started running towards Pripyat.

I arrived a few hours later, sweating in terror. The city was darker than usual. The wind was strong and visibility poor. I saw a silver minibus with its characteristic sky blue logo. A group of tourists were present at the site. They were probably exploring the surrounding buildings, no one was inside the vehicle except the driver. I tried to keep a low profile. After three weeks in the Zone, my appearance had become appalling. I had a shaggy beard and a nauseous smell. Even worse, I was starving. Thus, I had to steal food to survive.

I waited a few seconds, lurking in a bush. The driver of the minibus had not locked the doors. After all, no one was supposed to be there except the group of visitors. Why would you lock a door in a completely abandoned city?

The driver pulled himself out of the vehicle and took a few steps into the forest to urinate. I took advantage of this moment to discreetly enter the minibus and search the tourists' bags until I found a sandwich and a pack of cigarettes. I grabbed my loot and ran away in a hurry.

Once again, I tried to clear my head, to think calmly about this predicament I was facing. I had been wrong from the beginning. I had thought I was the instigator of our common treasure hunt. But in fact I was simply a cog, the abused pawn whose senses and weaknesses had been exploited by others.

Rightly so, my psychosis was now exacerbated. I was mentally visualising all the events since I entered the Zone, the meetings I had had, the places I had visited. I tried to organise my memories, to seek a meaning, some coherence to these events. Was there a more comprehensive plan? Perhaps I should go further back? Had I really come to the Zone on my own initiative, or was it the result of subtle incentives, of cleverly arranged manipulations?

From the beginning, Oleksandr had behaved strangely, with his apparent detachment constantly imbued with nervousness. He seemed to me tormented and cold, as if I were the cause of his concerns.

I myself had a certain uneasiness that remained unexplained. It is true that since childhood I had suffered from anxiety, nightmares, dizziness and other more or less disabling disorders. Temporary depressions too. Who hasn't had one before? Nevertheless, I had not always suffered in this way. I recalled the distant tranquility of my childhood in Pripyat.

The possibility of post-traumatic stress disorder hit me hard. The evacuations had triggered this syndrome in thousands of people, who were still suffering from various ailments. However, their condition was poorly recognised and rarely claimed. Some liquidators had brought actions against the European Court of Human Rights in order to obtain compensation. On the other hand, evacuees from Pripyat and the villages in the Zone had not received anything.

I tried to explore the origin of my failures, to make a study of my psyche. Andrei and Amanda were aware of my condition. Oleksandr also knew. He had noted my propensity to forget, but also my intuition skills. After all, I was the only one of us who had grown up in the Zone. The solution to the riddle was me. I had to locate and unlock Pripyat's treasure so they could appropriate it. Once the objective was reached, I would be discarded. My corpse would be easy to hide and no one would claim my body for an autopsy. My life didn't matter, my existence was ridiculous. Only what was buried in the depths of my memory mattered.

Oleksandr was clever, he had had a head start from the beginning. He probably knew my position right now or worse, maybe he was currently observing me.

Again, strong paranoia and headaches appeared. The sky was devilishly bright, which made me uncomfortable. I was out in the open, in the middle of a road skirting Pripyat.

I was trying to reach the forest to gain some discretion. Enveloped by trees, I tried to think. Amanda was dead, Andrei had run away. Only Oleksandr and I were left. Was he acting alone now? Maybe he had an accomplice? I thought of the Babushka, Egor, the Howler...

I was torn by hesitation. My options were dubious. Leave the Zone and end this nightmare or complete this scavenger hunt that only I had the solution to? What did I have left? I could dive into the icy water of the river and never come out. Hanging was also possible. The trees were legion and their long branches were spread like evil arms, diabolical temptations. These invitations to die were taunting me. No, I was better than that.

***

I walked on the rails, crushing with my feet anything that blocked my progress. Yanov was very close. The station had opened in the 1920s and had once served Moscow. I arrived at a large vacant plot of land. Soviet military equipment was stored there, destined to be forgotten. Some MDK-2Ms were lying in amongst some other vehicles in an advanced state of abandonment. The caterpillars were still present although they were worn. The numbering painted on the bodywork could still be seen.

A few train carcasses lay rotting. I remembered my walk with Andrei. I was unable to recognise the car he had shown me. There were several , most of them similar looking and decayed. As I considered the locomotives, I was struck by a red star painted on one of the carriages. It was one of the most famous figures of communism with its pentagram form, which was supposed to represent a lot of things according to interpretations. Today, the pictogram was accepted as a symbol of popular culture, so much so that it was proudly displayed by some well-known alcohol brands, to the annoyance of the former Eastern Bloc countries.

The red was so bright that it almost attacked the eyes. Someone had probably had some fun and redesigned it. The painting, regardless of its quality, could not have survived three decades without losing its brilliance. I had been dwelling on this detail for several minutes when someone gently tapped me on the shoulder.

'Am I disturbing you?'

It was Oleksandr. I jumped back.

'I'm a little surprised to see you here. I thought you had returned to Kiev,' I replied.

'Yes, I did too, but I missed the Zone. Kiev is pretty dull right now. Is everything all right?'

'All right. Yes, I'm fine, though I'm pretty tired these days.'

'Have you met any people lately, besides Andrei?'

'No, no, no.'

'And what are you doing here? Are you looking to see or find something special?'

'Oh nothing, I'm wandering. I'm going to leave soon.'

He cleared his throat as if he disapproved of my answer. His peremptory tone annoyed me. I felt like I was being interrogated, it wasn't a friendly discussion.

'All right, don't hesitate to call me if you see or hear anything strange. I'm your protector, don't forget. I feel responsible. After all, I was the one who showed you how to get in. I don't want anything to happen to you.'

'Everything will be fine, I plan to come back out soon anyway.'

'Very well. I'll see you later.'

He left as quickly as he had appeared, his silhouette gradually disappearing, caught up in the falling snow. Once again, Oleksandr had found himself in the area. The coincidences followed one another and made me uncomfortable. I had the impression that he knew where I was without even looking for me. He appeared unexpectedly and seemed to invent a combination of circumstances to explain it. I was beginning to think he was following me. But how could he know my movements so precisely? I had no transmitter or emergency beacon.   I started to unpack my bag and meticulously search the contents. One particular object caught my attention. The Geiger counter that Oleksandr gave me on the first day was there. It must have contained a GPS chip. Naively, I had kept it with me. Thus,

Oleksandr had been following me from the beginning. He was informed of all my movements. Maybe he even inserted a microphone or even a camera? He could have listened to all my conversations. I was now sure: he knew about Amanda. A shudder ran through my body, making my organs and the ground under my feet vibrate.

Why did he need me? What was his interest in manipulating me?

Deep inside me lay an obvious solution. I couldn't grasp it, as if the truth was too obvious to emerge clearly.

***

Silence. I was lying against a wall, my eyes half-closed and my hands joined on my chest. The ground was cold, but my body was fine there. My mind was wandering. Strange imaginings were attacking me. I was in a state of near sleep, my muscles resting and my attention relaxed. I could see shadows, but I couldn't determine if they were dreamed of or suspended above me. I could feel my fatigue catching up with me. Slowly, almost gently, I fell asleep. It was at this moment that he appeared. Two powerful hands fell on my throat and began to squeeze methodically. Panicked, I opened my eyes in a hurry. I couldn't distinguish my attacker. He wore a hood that concealed his face. I squirmed in all directions to escape his embrace, beating him with what I hoped were very violent blows. My attacker was neither strong nor fit for this type of combat. I felt that his own pain made him doubtful. His actions were now insecure, almost trembling. Diminished by my attacks, he finally let go and fled without saying a word. The attack lasted less than ten seconds. His retreat had been pitiful, the assailant had left as quickly as he had emerged. As for me, I was breathless; I could not pursue him. Once again, I found myself huddled in my meagre shelter, subjected to a state of absolute terror. Death had sought to strike, once again. Someone else wanted to get rid of me. In the fight, I had managed to pull out a few blond hairs, too pure a colour to be natural. It only took me a few seconds and the moon's dim light to understand the identity of my attacker. Deep down, I wasn't really surprised. I had always known that. I hoped not to forget this moment, I promised myself I would freeze it forever in my memory. I lay down again against the wall. Silence.

Chapter 12 — Epitaph

32nd day in the Zone, Wednesday.

It was a gray afternoon, as often in the Zone. After going through the forest maze, I arrived at the Howler's hut. I hailed him with a loud voice. An icy silence was my only answer. No matter how much I shouted, or threw rocks, he didn't answer.

Perhaps he had simply secluded himself?

It was his way, after all. The Howler had probably barricaded himself in his house. The suspended ladder had been folded up and there was no way I could reach it. The only solution was to climb the tree trunk. But that was unthinkable. Not even a bear could have climbed that high. I was thinking the worst. Maybe he'd killed himself. I ruled out the possibility of his murder. He had distanced himself from human interactions. No one had any real reason to kill him. At least, not that I was aware of.

I mustered my courage and ran for the tree with both hands. My fingers grabbed the first branches and I carefully began the ascent. Despite the lack of handholds, the climb seemed much easier than Duga had been. The wind was harmless. It seemed to almost accompany me, gently, holding its breath. I felt safe and out of danger. However, I was not held by any harness. A simple loss of balance and I would plummet. That would be the end. However, I was not frightened by the possibility of my own destruction. I had been through so much recently that I had detached myself from death. It was just one shadow among many. It would hit me sooner or later, anticipating it wouldn't change anything. I cleared my thoughts in order to concentrate on my progress, trying to make the right movements without losing the rhythm of my climbing.

When I reached the top of the tree, I grabbed the iron bar that marked the entrance to the cabin, with its small porch fitted with a few boards. There were a few noticeable footprints, cut sharply into the snow, suggesting that they were recent.

The cabin door was ajar. I didn't bother knocking to signal my presence. An abhorrent smell was coming from inside. Slowly, I approached, entering the house with muffled steps. Where the hell was he?

I spotted him quite quickly. The Howler was sitting in his only chair in a strange position. His body seemed deformed. His head had been cut off and his arms dismembered. His chest was covered in blood and showed multiple lacerations. I felt myself gag, and was overcome with dizziness. He had been massacred, obviously without having been able to put up any defence. I couldn't stand this sight any longer. His tortured body disgusted me. I couldn't stay there. I went out with shaking hands. Outside, the blizzard echoed my pain. Rage stirred me more than fear. I threw the suspended ladder down to the ground and clambered down at high speed. Once on the ground, I started cutting strips and gathering a few centimetres of rope. I put it all in my pocket, storing the precious commodity.

My last ally in the Zone had gone. I found myself alone and helpless. It would be so easy for me to run away, to put an end to this brutal nightmare. But my will prevented me from doing so. A part of me refused fiercely to give up. The Zone had trapped me. I was no longer in control of my decisions. Various emotions were intertwined. It was difficult to appease them. Sadness and anger dominated fear. More particularly, a need for revenge had been born in me that I felt right down to my bowels. My face was too tense to cry. I took long breaths, hoping that they would help me to think, to come to the wisest decision possible. I couldn't help it: Oleksandr had to pay.

I took one last look at the shack and then left. On the way, I thought someone might have followed me. I remembered the drone and the phone threats. The Howler's hideout was probably under surveillance and I could be being tracked by some enemy at this very moment. I had to organise my getaway.

The snow had stopped falling, my steps were no longer masked. I decided to take off my shoes in order to limit my tracks, and continued simply equipped with socks. My feet were soaked and bitten by the cold. I ignored these feelings. I didn't want anyone to follow me. I wanted to survive a little longer, to prolong my existence in the Zone. I went up the forest towards Pripyat with my knife in hands. He was supposed to be there, he was supposed to be waiting for me. Thinking of Oleksandr made my jaw clench and my teeth grind.

I arrived in Pripyat with an impetuous mind. I walked the roads from one side of the street to the other, looking for my rival. I wandered openly, ostensibly roaming in the middle of the roads without taking any precautions. Three hours passed. I had criss-crossed most of the city and there was no trace of Oleksandr or anyone else. The night was slowly approaching and I didn't want to sleep in Pripyat. I no longer trusted its dark buildings, its vacant properties where I had almost lost my life. Contrary to any logic, I decided to spend the night outside. I chose the Pripyat stadium. The structure was completely overgrown with vegetation, only a few brave stands remained overlooking the vacant lot. The wild beasts did not frighten me. The dark night no longer scared me. I fell asleep serenely, rocked by the caresses of the wind.

In the early morning, I was awakened by countless clicks. I opened my eyes painfully and saw several people in the vicinity. A group of individuals was there. They were tourists accompanied by their guide. Most of them were equipped with cutting-edge cameras and imperial-looking telephoto lenses. They spoke German, Turkish and English. Some of them were staring at me with naive curiosity. Others seemed suspicious. When I saw them, I suddenly got up, giving hostile looks. I noticed that the guide kept his hand under his jacket, probably ready to draw a gun, in case I turned violent.

As I continued to observe the small group, one of the tourists photographed me very closely. He approached me with a rather quiet and natural step. He acted as if he expected no reaction. The guy took not one, but many shots, using his camera in continuous mode. I was irritated by the flashes produced by the device. I imagined my face in the centre of his little viewfinder, while he was at work adjusting the right parameters. His picture had to be sharp. I remained impassive, although I was boiling with rage. The tourist came towards me holding a khaki-coloured gas mask with a red light on top. He had a satisfied smile that made him despicable.

'Could you wear this please?'

When they heard his query, the others laughed. My brain was numbed with cold and fear. It took me several seconds to understand his request. Contradictory thoughts attacked me. Should I agree to be turned into a freak? Should I make a fool of myself in front of all these people, stage myself in this place where so many people had fought and suffered from radiation? Or on the contrary, should I grab the object which was being held out to me, and launch it back at its owner? Break his nose, beat him up when he was on the ground until he was begging in agony?

Obviously, the guide understood that I was considering this second option. My face had hardened, my jaw had tightened and my heart was pounding. The guide approached and put his hand on the tourist's shoulder:

'Enough, we're going back to the minibus.'

The small group obeyed without protest. One by one, they turned their heels and walked away in a single line. As they turned back, one of them took one last picture of me. He was the one who asked me to pose. He always had the same sarcastic look. I picked up a stone that I hoped would be sharp enough and slowly walked towards the minibus. The guide was young and obviously did not expect this kind of reaction. He urged everyone to get up quickly. The vehicle started in a hurry, leaving me in a cloud of black smoke, still armed with my makeshift weapon. I suddenly saw one of the passengers giving me the finger through the window. Instinctively, I threw the stone in his direction, hitting the side of the minibus, but without causing much damage. Already, the vehicle was disappearing in the midst of the smoke, and I was left alone in the company of my anger.

Given the terror I had inspired, I imagined it was unlikely that the incident would end there. Guided tours had to be secure, tourist safety was important for business to continue to flourish. My threatening behaviour and unauthorised presence would be reported. I would probably be hunted down by a gang of Ukrainian soldiers and removed from the Zone. I would rot in a jail. This time, no bribe would save me. The scene had probably been filmed by other tourists. I would end up on the Internet, the sequence would be edited and spread through the different platforms. The video would be shared by thousands of simple-minded people on social networks, that would go around the world in a few hours. Yes, I was risking a lot.

I imagined a hunt with a team looking for me, dogs barking at me, helicopters spinning in the sky to track my position. I could already hear the sound of the walkie-talkies, the screams of the sirens and the echoes of gun-shots. They would catch me and leave me in a cell full of excrement, giving off a pungent smell. I didn't deserve much better.

The headache was resurfacing, more vicious, more intense than ever. I could feel my brains imploding. I placed snow on my forehead to try to relieve the pain. It was only getting worse. My breathing was noisy and jerky. I had not forgotten my main enemy. The suffering had not dispelled my hatred. Oleksandr had to pay. He would die tonight.

***

The night was imminent, darkness would soon fall on the Zone. I arrived at the small church of St-Elias. This place was notorious for having escaped radioactive cont-amination, it was a miraculous anecdote that the religious liked to spread. Divine authorities had spared the place be-cause of the prayers of the local pope. Thus, in the vicinity of the church, the thresholds of radioactivity were more than three times lower than those in Kiev. But, I had not come to meditate, I had a sinister task to complete.

I had no difficulty in locating him. I knew where he was. I always knew. My steps guided me while my brain ignored the path.

Oleksandr was there, leaning against a palisade. He seemed to have been waiting for me, or at least he had an-ticipated my coming to this place so much that he didn't seem surprised to see me. He waved at me to come closer. Did he want to negotiate? I had to be cautious.

I approached slowly, head held high as if I was trying to measure up my opponent. When I got to where he was, I kept a distance of a few metres. This guy was mad, so he was unpredictable. I had to be cautious. Nevertheless, I ostensibly had a defiant look on my face. I wanted to show him that I wasn't afraid of him. I had hardened up. The Zone had made me more experienced.

'So what's new?' he asked in a slightly provocative tone.

'Shut up! I warned Andrei about your schemes. He doesn't trust you either. We have had enough. I will talk to Amanda about it. In fact, we are considering...'

He interrupted me:

'Stop it, you know very well that Amanda is dead.'

My breathing accelerated. I knew it, of course, I knew it. But I had a doubt, a terrifying doubt.

'When? When? Who?!' I exclaimed.

'A fortnight ago. Her body was found in the forest to the north. Someone took care of burying her.'

My pulse was pounding.

'Who would want to hurt her? How is that possible?'

Oleksandr turned his head, looking confused and sincerely saddened. I called him again:

'Look at me! Look at me! Explain it to me!'

'Andrei warned me. He didn't give me any more details.'

'I will find him, yes I will find him!' I shouted in a raspy voice.

'I don't know if you can trust him.'

'What do you mean?'

'Andrei and Amanda have been lying to you from the beginning. They are not looking for the treasure. Or at least, I think they've already found it, as we all have.'

'Fuck you!' I shouted.

'He is also not from the bourgeoisie of Kiev. His father was a miner, one of those who had been requisitioned to build the underground gallery under the reactor. As for you, you're not a journalist.'

My blood circulation accelerated. He knew. His tranquillity contrasted with my state of tension.

'I made a phone call to your supposed editorial office. They've never heard of you. You're not very bright for a forger. Although, you have a great talent for betraying yourself.'

'Fuck you, man. Fuck you.'

'You're angry and that's normal. I would be just as upset if I were you. Do you even remember when we met? The circumstances were banal, but I remember every detail.'

'Shut up! Shut up! If you get any closer, I'll kill you.'

He took a step forward. Oleksandr seemed totally indifferent to my warnings.

'Look, I think we need to talk.'

'I don't want to see you anymore,' I replied.

'Yes, of course. Of course, you forgot again.'

He put his hands on his face and scratched his beard. He was pretending to have some kind of compassion for me. It was a bluff. I imagined him wielding a gun any minute now.

'Don't move! Don't move!'

'You know, we have more in common than you suspect. I immediately understood when I met you. I immediately detected in you this weakness that is eating away at you. Everyone has detected it. I guess you're not fully aware of it. Or at least, you may know about it, but you lose the memory as soon as you have created it. Amnesia is consuming you, depriving you of your own history. This mental illness is hindering your search for identity. Your spatial and temporal landmarks are fragile, your concentration is precarious, your nights are tumultuous. For more than thirty years, you've been going through hell... I've tried to look after you, to protect you from the Zone. I couldn't stop you, I knew you were inevitably attracted to it... Now you're tormented. All your memories, all your actions form an incoherent mixture, a memory porridge that you are unable to restore. You have lived through every single one of these moments, including a murder.'

As he pronounced his words, I perceived his discreet movements in my direction. He seemed to be approaching while trying to hide his intentions.

Suddenly, I warned him:

'Step back! Step back!'

'I haven't moved,' he objected.

I drew my weapon.

'I swear I'll shoot you if you get any closer!'

Oleksandr sighed. He had a little smile on his face.

'Oh, yeah? I'm waiting.'

He took a step forward with an air of challenge. It was too much. Instinctively, I pulled the trigger and closed my eyes. I already visualised Oleksandr collapsing in a pool of blood. He would be nothing more than a common corpse destined for putrefaction and oblivion. However, nothing happened except a squeaky click, indicating my failure. Obviously, the gun didn't work.

'Let me help you with that.'

'I don't need you.'

Oleksandr seemed totally indifferent to my reactions. He reached out his hand to me as a sign of appeasement and advanced. We were now so close that I could see my own reflection in his pupil. With all my strength, I struck the pistol's butt against his head. The shock was memorable. I saw him collapse like a stone, his head bloody and his body disjointed. He wouldn't move anymore. Oleksandr was destroyed.

I immediately fled, running on the path, smashing the branches that were blocking my way. Despite the feeling of tiredness, I was boiling with anger. A new energy was spreading in my body.

How many times had I experienced this feeling?

I spent my time escaping, surviving, struggling with the elements. Oleksandr was probably perishing in the snow by now. He may have been tough, but the cold would take its toll. His brain would trigger a vasoconstriction that would increase his heart rate to maintain his body temperature, but that would not be enough. His heart would eventually give up. His death would not hurt much in the end. The rifle butt must have knocked him out. He would lose his life in his unconsciousness, unaware of the great journey he was about to make.

I had given him the luckiest end of all. An end that I envied.

Chapter 13 — Estrapade

34th day in the Zone.

Oleksandr looked at me with an impenetrable and icy gaze. His gray eyes were inexpressive. He drew his weapon and fired without saying anything. I had run away the second I saw him bury his hand in his anorak. I knew he would hunt me down, he would not give up anything, until he annihilated me and my memory into dust.

Our pursuit was unusual, in the sense that it was perfectly silent. No words or threats had been uttered. He didn't need to express his intention to kill me. I knew from the fraction of a second that our eyes crossed that one of us was going to die. A smell of death was floating in the air.

I didn't understand what was going on. I didn't have time for that. I had imagined him destroyed, I thought I was free. He came out of nowhere, like a ghost returning from beyond the grave. I thought I had killed him two days ago, I thought I was done with him. But even now, I had to run away.

My physical condition was much better than his, but Oleksandr was driven by a kind of evil energy like that which characterises individuals who are not afraid of death. He must have felt invincible. Nothing could stop him, his strength was tenfold.

I was pretending to run blindly, but I had an idea. I knew where to bring him. Oleksandr could not use his gun near the reactor. The noise would be too easily recognisable and surveillance cameras would identify it. Security services would be able to intercept him before he could leave the Zone. So he would have to kill me with his hands. Maybe he had a knife? Maybe he was planning to slit my throat?

I was only a few metres ahead, I was in good range. I had to be quick, my chances of survival were reduced every second. I was running towards the reactor, directing my course and trying to find the right path. The night was clear, it would be easy for me to spot what I was looking for. Oleksandr was so focused in his determination that he would not see it. He was chasing me, probably unaware that I had a plan.

I saw my objective. It was right on my path. When it came, I jumped discreetly to avoid it. My stride had been light enough to dodge the obstacle without alerting my attacker. I counted endless seconds in my head, thinking the worst. I finally heard the thumping sound I was expecting and turned around. Oleksandr remained on the ground, his arms spread out and his leg bloody. The barbed wire had trapped him.

I approached him, suspicious, but determined to get it over with. I was physically diminished by the days of effort, deprivation and nights spent outside, but my survival instinct spurred my strength. Fear and rage multiplied the intensity of my punches. I kicked him hard, disfiguring what was left of his face. Blood spurted and splashed onto the ice patches around us. I was determined to reduce him to a pulp. But Oleksandr was tough and fought hard. It was difficult for me to struggle on with his sturdy build and his apparent indifference to his own pain.

The silence of our battle contrasted with its prodigious violence. Oleksandr hadn't even screamed when he met the barbed wire. He had remained impassive, absorbed in his murderous madness. He was hiding his suffering, but I knew I had weakened him. On the other hand, I felt that he was getting back on top. If he could get up, I wouldn't have a chance.

I grabbed the fence that was strewn all over the ground and used it to strangle Oleksandr. Carefully, I pressed it against his throat, squeezing as hard as my muscles allowed. My fingers were bloody, the iron points were sinking through my gloves, slashing my skin. Insensitive to my pain, I maintained the pressure. Oleksandr's face was paler and more and more tense, I felt that the end was near. His blood was no longer flowing, and despite the night, I could perfectly distinguish his ghostly skin tone. He tried to say a word. His lips trembled as if ready to formulate their final syllables. I finished it off with an uppercut to the temple. Blood diffused under the skin where I had struck. Oleksandr was no longer struggling and was not exhaling any breath. He was covered with bruises. His breathing had stopped, his eyes had definitely closed. This time it was for good.

I got up and fled without further delay, still dizzy with the outpouring of violence that had taken place. Already, a dark and familiar paranoia was rising in me. I was convinced that I would be found. Oleksandr's allies would seek revenge.

I wanted to get rid of my bloody gloves. I didn't even know if the blood that covered them came from me or Oleksandr. I filled them with a few stones and threw them into the river below. Breathlessly, I retreated into the forest.

My legs were shaking, making me lose my balance. I had killed a family man with my own fists and a barbed wire. My bloodthirsty instinct had gone wild and I had taken a life. What kind of guy had I become?

The Zone had made me unconscious of my actions while exacerbating my violence. Oleksandr had certainly attacked me, he had wanted to kill me. But I could have fled, left the Zone once and for all, gone back to Vienna and put an end to these miserable events. However, I had decided to stay and kill him. I no longer knew who had pursued whom, who was the real enemy in the Zone. Oleksandr, Amanda and the Howler had perished. Now it was just me and Andrei left. At this point, he must have fled far enough away to escape me. He had put chance on his side. The scoundrel! The most harmless of all...

***

I hurried on, ignoring my sore legs and the biting cold. I was thinking rapidly: 'The hospital basement, the invincible door ... it was obvious.'

I rushed through the forest, crossing ravines, dodging branches. I only had one name in mind: Kopatchi.

I remembered the meeting with Oleksandr. Had I really hit him hard enough? Had I managed to strangle him as I wanted? Yes, I think this time I had done it. I was convinced I had killed him. He had to be murdered twice, the guy was so tough. Now I was convinced, he would slowly rot, devoured by worms. I hadn't come back to Kopatchi for the sake of his memory. I had something to recover, something very desirable.

The building I was looking for was easy to spot. It was of medium size and rather precarious, its shape contrasted with the surrounding houses.

The kindergarten had a basement that had never been used before. It had partially collapsed and access was difficult. I took the flashlight and stole through a small broken window. The place was disgusting and repulsive, so it was perfect to hide what I was looking for.

I started crawling in the dirt, avoiding the rotten wooden planks. The gaps let in light and revealed columns of radioactive dust that put me on guard. I finally spotted the little purple canvas bag. It was buried and almost invisible. I was short of breath and my lungs were full of dust. I fingered my discovery, caressing its purple case, as if it contained a sacred relic. My fingers could detect the key that resided within it. I had succeeded.

I now had to attempt to get out of this filthy place. Everything around me was stinking and desolate. I finally managed to get out. I was covered with dirt, snow and filth.

A distant noise came to me. I heard discussions in English. Tourists were approaching, I didn't want to meet them. I brushed my clothes off one last time before fleeing through the trees.

I had to locate Andrei, ask him for help. Only he would know how to get into the hospital in Pripyat and access the damn corridor.

I decided to return to the railway line near Yanov, where his charming car was located. As I expected, Andrei was hanging around there. He was true to himself, with his detached look and his cigarette in his mouth. Noticing my swollen look and bloody hands, he called out to me:

'Is Oleksandr dead?'

'I killed him,' I replied laconically.

'Admirable.'

He punched me in the face and knocked me down. His punch was so hard that he must have been planning it. I rolled on the ground, breathless and vomiting blood. He held out a hand to me, then helped me up before hitting me again, this time in the chest. I collapsed once again. I was too weak to react. I was only enduring, I no longer wanted to fight.

Andrei stooped down to my height and gazed at me. His eyes were shining like lamps. He sketched a smile, revealing his lower jaw and a line of yellowed teeth. He picked up the little purple bag that had fallen out of my pocket. Disgust overwhelmed me.

'I would never have succeeded without you, thank you my friend!'

It was with these last words that he vanished, abandoning me to my regrets and a hatred that I knew was insurmountable. Andrei had the key. He had spared me with a smile, but I would have preferred him to kill me with a dagger.

I got up as best I could, struggling to regain my senses. The air was heavy, suitable for the turmoil that was occurring. I tried to reassure myself, to hold on to some hope. Tears came to my cheeks. I was exhausted and grieving.   Suddenly, I fell to my knees, contracting all my muscles until I constricted my breathing. My lungs were still panting but my throat was tight with fear. I took one last breath.

My howl pierced the trees and was heard throughout the entire Zone. It interrupted the flow of rivers and swept away the murmurs of the wind. For a moment, I was able to interfere with the passage of time. I had stopped the elements and conquered nature in an unparalleled roar. For a moment, I felt victorious in a fight that I had never stopped losing. In that very tiny second, I had finally been able to triumph, exult and abolish the rage that had been bleeding in me for too long.

Unfortunately, slowly, silence came again, destroying my cry, my survival.

Chapter 14 — Memories of Kiev

5 February, first discoveries of the city.

The night was clear and strewn with subtle clouds. I was wandering in Kiev with a relaxed mind. I particularly appreciated the evening atmosphere punctuated by a few light breezes, which slipped at regular intervals. Despite the late hour, the heat was still heavy and strolling around the Dnieper was very pleasant.

I headed downtown. Bands of teenagers wandered the streets, armed with portable speakers, cigarettes and balls. On Kontrakova Square, the Ferris wheel split the sky to the sound of quite boisterous pop music. Many onlookers were outside, some were walking their dogs, others, like me, were wandering the streets at random. The shops were shutting down. The atmosphere was serene and joyful, in contrast to the bloody conflict in the east. The people of Kiev did not live the same life as the rest of the country. Of course, by western standards, they were very poor; however, they did not risk their lives, they did not experience the daily horror of an imminent bombardment. The torments of war affected them, but did not threaten them directly. Here and there the Ukrainian flag was proudly standing, often alongside that of the European Union as a sign of its attachment. I remained pensive about these symbolisms.

I finally choose to go up Saint-André street. It was beautiful and winding, it looked like a staircase to Olympus. I walked quietly through it, admiring the various coloured facades before noticing a rather flashy bar. It had a striking appearance.

I pushed open the door, determined to quench my thirst. The interior was less flashy than the frontage. The bar was very dark and a musty smell scattered throughout the area. I felt uncomfortable, ready to turn around. But the appeal of a drink was too strong. I sat down at the counter and ordered a Chernigovsky. American punk from the '90s was ringing in the bar's speakers. To my left, a bunch of jerks were sitting at the table and playing cards loudly. As my drink arrived, a tall fellow patted me on the back and sat next to me. He shook my hand and introduced himself soberly.

'Oleksandr, nice to meet you.'

The man was strong. His poorly shaved and his grayish beard suggested that he was in his forties. This feeling was reinforced by the presence of many wrinkles on his forehead. His skin betrayed a tired and afflicted soul. His steel blue eyes were severe. That was the kind of gaze that dark-minded men have. Probably because he was caught up in remorse. His eyes must have seen all kinds of things, testifying to a life of hardship and renunciation.

He started the conversation and told me about himself. He often came here after work, he knew anecdotes about all the customers at the bar.

Oleksandr's behaviour was somewhat bipolar. He would easily go from small friendly pats on the shoulder to dark looks and cold taciturn lines. We spoke in English. I didn't want to tell him my Ukrainian origins. Our discussion diverged from my trip to Ukraine. I informed Oleksandr of my intentions to visit the Zone. He listened to me without blinking, almost religiously. He never tried to interrupt me. He just stared at me while drinking his beer silently. He didn't seem surprised by my approach.

I asked him for advice.

'I can take you there,' he said soberly.

'Seriously? When?'

'Tomorrow if you want.'

'It's that simple? Can we really get there?'

'Yes.'

'When will we leave?'

'We'll go at dawn. The roads are in poor condition, it will take us time to get there.'

'What do I need?'

'Nothing at all. Your shoes will do the job. I'll provide the rest.'

'Do we need special authorisation? And how much does it cost?'

'No. No. We'll enter illegally, you won't have to pay anything. I know how to do it.'

'But ... have you ever been?'

'Yes, many times. I know the Zone perfectly well.'

He had responded in a destabilising way as if my question was not justified because the solution was so obvious. My mind was lost in an opaque mist, I tried to imagine what would happen next day. Oleksandr slapped my shoulder and approached to pierce me with his gaze.

He whispered:

'One last thing. Are you afraid?'

'No. No,' I stammered.

'Um... All right ... that's better.'

He stared at me for a few more seconds without speaking, embarrassing me. He seemed surprised, but satisfied. His face had an air of mystery.

'Be in Maidan Square at 6:00AM tomorrow morning. Don't bring too much stuff with you. And above all, don't tell anyone about our little plan.'

He smiled at me and then walked out of the bar slamming the door. I was a little unsettled by his sudden disappearance. I paid for our drinks and also set off to my hotel. Tomorrow, the expedition would begin.

The night turned out to be short and difficult. I didn't know if my restless sleep was paralysed by fear or euphoria. Probably both. I was going to revisit the place of my childhood. A radioactive space condemned for eternity, a space that had seen me born and to which I would be bound until my last breath. Images of Pripyat were already floating in my mind. A lost city, alabaster and perilous territories. The promise of a unique experience was on the horizon.

Sleep was elusive. Around 4:00 a.m., I finally slumbered as the first light of day began to dawn.

The alarm clock rang suddenly. I got up in a flash, without a struggle. I was carried by my excitement and prepared for everything that would come my way.

I scrupulously finished my packing, silent and solemn. Oleksandr had asked me to bring the bare minimum. I had to trust his advice, he who was taking risks for me. I weighed the package one last time. Perfect. I was ready.

I walked out of the building and closed the door slowly, with a little smile on my face. A shiver of excitement ran through me as I walked down the snow-covered alleyway.

The adventure looked beautiful and scary. I was rushing towards it without fear or restraint.

Acknowledgements

This book would not have been possible without the precious advice and sweet personality of Vika, my Ukrainian guide, whom I am now sure has not revealed all the secrets of Pripyat to me. In addition to a visit on the site, many musical influences helped me to develop this story. In particular, I must thank Steve Reich and Alessandro Cortini, whose sound layers have always inspired me throughout the writing process. It would also be selfish to end these lines without mentioning Vanessa, Maliia, Tomek, Ingrid and many others who advised me, supported me or only knew me during the writing of this book. Finally, I thank Abby Button for her valuable proofreading and help in order to improve the translation.

If you enjoyed this book, feel free to give me a review on Amazon, it's important for me as it is my debut novel. For anyone who would like to comment, criticise this novel or simply exchange opinions about the *Zone*, it is also possible to contact the author directly through

Emails: amaury.dreher@gmail.com

Instagram: @Toskalahti

Finally, you should know that a sequel is planned for this novel :).

The Lagom Project

Following a citizens' initiative, a global collective was created to transcribe the memories of humanity in the throes of collapse. The decline in biodiversity, the paralysis of thought and the brutal transformation of a world in agony make us fear the worst. Civilisation would be living its last moments. Thousands of citizens have chosen to participate in a memorial project and share their memories. Prophets of doom or decisive witnesses of a new mutation? Five characters through their feelings evoke these planetary events that shaped the 21st century. Come and experience the Collapse through this news of anticipation!

(The Lagom Project - Amaury Dreher, 2020)

The Delicacy of Dreams

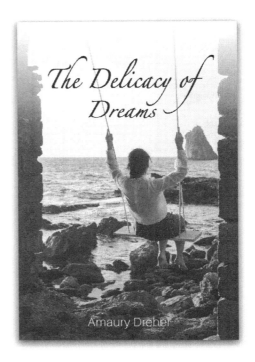

A young architect embarks on a promising career. From Beirut to Kathmandu, from New York to Istanbul, Nathan Levine is continuing his travels which will help him fulfil his dreams and regain lost happiness. Encounters and peregrinations lead him to constantly change the course of his life. What is he trying to escape from? A consummate love? An evaporated family life?

Lily is a gifted but sensitive actress. Faced with multiple dramas, she will have to constantly reinvent herself. Between dreams and disillusions: how to soften the vacillations of a life?

A human epic in a contemporary world that is at once marvellous, cruel and unpredictable.

(The Delicacy of Dreams - Amaury Dreher, 2020)

Legal Deposit: March 2019

Independently published.

Made in the USA
Las Vegas, NV
01 August 2021

27399311R00118